OPERATION BLACK SWAN

OWEN PARR

A JOHN POWERS NOVEL

OPERATION
BLACK SWAN

Title: Operation Black Swan

Author: Owen Parr

Published by: Owen Parr

www.owenparr.net, owen@owenparr.com

Other fictional novel by Owen Parr: Due Diligence

ISBN-13 978-1519178220
ISBN-10: 1519178220

Published in United States

To all present and past members of

The United States Armed Forces.

Thank you for your service and unselfish dedication to our country.

To my grandchildren:

Robbie, Dylan, Logan and Cameron.

You guys are the pilot light that keeps my fire burning.

I love you!

Papu.

Prologue

In 1983 a Korean Airlines 747, flight 007, was shot down by the Soviet Union. Aboard that flight was an outspoken congressman by the name of Larry P. McDonald.

In 1976 Congressman McDonalds said: *"The drive of the Rockefellers and their allies is to create a one-world government combining supercapitalism and Communism under the same tent, all under their control. Do I mean there is a conspiracy? Yes I do. I am convinced there is such a plot, international in scope, generations old in planning, and incredibly evil in intent."*

David Rockefeller, in his book Memoir, said the following: *"Some even believe we are part of a secret cabal working against the United States, characterizing my family and me as 'internationalists' and of conspiring with others around the world to build a more integrated global and political structure – one world, if you will. If that's the charge, I stand guilty, and I am proud of it."*

"Increasingly, the Chinese will own a lot more of the world because they will be converting their dollar reserves and U.S. government bonds into real assets."

– George Soros

CHAPTER ONE

2002

Mexico City, Mexico

"John, where are you now?" asked Alex, as I answered his call with my new gadget, a wireless headset and earbud.

"Boss, I'm at the San Angel Inn Restaurant in Mexico City," I replied.

"Have you acquired our targets?" Alex asked.

"I am looking at three Cuban officials meeting with three Chinese officials in a private dining room," I said, crossing my legs and raising the newspaper that I was pretending to read so it would cover my face.

"Are you exposed?" asked Alex.

"Not my first rodeo, Boss. I am hiding in plain sight, just sitting in this beautiful courtyard by a historical fountain, taking in some rays from the sun, and actually listening to the chirping of a mockingbird. It's a beautiful day here in Mexico City, temperature of 70 degrees and blue skies. This courtyard has a perfect view of the restaurant's L-shaped configuration," I explained to Alex. It was probably too much information. He liked details short and succinct, not with a lot of flowery descriptions. But I enjoyed annoying people occasionally, especially when I'm bored.

"But they can see you," Alex insisted.

"They can see Father Thomas sitting in the courtyard, not John Powers. I am wearing my priestly disguise. I've never been made as Father Thomas. Hopefully, no one here dies and I am asked to administer last rites. Then I'll be screwed," I replied, laughing. "I'll call you later from the hotel, Boss." I hung up the phone and picked up on the aroma of the red mole sauce they were serving a few yards away. Damn, I was hungry. I tended to get a little sarcastic and flippant when I was bored and hungry. Watching six foreigners eating a Mexican lunch was boring. Don't get me wrong. This was much better than sitting at a desk somewhere analyzing something.

A waiter kept coming over and asking if he could get me anything. He had already told me about the restaurant's historic site. He said the Florentine marble fountain next to the courtyard where I sat looking at the Cuban and Chinese officials, had been the same location where horses owned by Pancho Villa and Emiliano Zapata had drunk water in 1914. Villa and Zapata had been generals in the Mexican revolution of the early 1900s and had stopped at the hacienda to divide Mexico into north and south territories for themselves. Sitting there, I could envision these guys and their horses. I could only imagine what the smell was like then, with all the horses around this fountain. I wasn't hungry anymore.

I had joined Alex a year ago at Sect-Intel Group. Having developed a heart murmur after three years as an operative for the CIA and the Department of Defense, in a group that will go nameless for lack of a better name, I was given a desk job, an analyst job. I wanted no part of it. No sir, not me. Sitting at a desk was not something I could do for more than, five minutes, give or take four. So I retired, took my disability pay, and joined Alex to continue my passion for covert operations. His legal department made me sign a waiver. I guess if I croaked during an operation due to my heart, I'd better die quick because these attorneys were not going to give me shit. I signed. At thirty-two years old, I was still a free spirit and full of life. There would be time later to slow down and maybe chase that little white ball around luscious greenery with other silly-clad old men.

Prior to joining the CIA, I had spent nine years with Delta Force, a Special Forces group of the United States Army. I had served in Operation Gothic Serpent, part of the Battle for Mogadishu, where two Black Hawk helicopters had been shot down in 1993. This operation had taken a toll on me, as it did on many of the Americans fighting there at that time. An operation that had been intended to take about one hour resulted in eighteen of my guys—American soldiers—dead and roughly seventy-three wounded. Delta, together with SEALs, Air Force para-rescue men, and others, found us in a battle for our lives. The goal of the operation had been to capture two lieutenants of the self-proclaimed president of Somalia, General Mohamed Farrah Hassan Aidid. Thousands of Somali militiamen compounded the problems after the helicopters crashed. Two Delta Force snipers, close friends of mine, had volunteered to hold off the militia during the night until help arrived the next day. Unfortunately, the militia overran them. Another one of my guys, a Delta fighter, was killed in a mortar attack in the morning as our American forces found ourselves in urban-style warfare. It was reported that somewhere between 1,500 to 3,000 Somalis died during the battle, but that was not enough to relieve the grief experienced by all the American personnel involved in the fierce fight. No amount of casualties on the enemy's side would have been enough.

Now I was part of a growing industry, an industry of private security and intelligence companies contracting with the U.S. government, other friendly governments, and private as well as public companies. The unfortunate attack on the Twin Towers in New York City on September 11, 2001, had most of the U.S. intelligence community concentrating on counterterrorism. Operations not directly involved with counterterrorism were contracted out to private firms such as Alex's Sect-Intel Group, which I had joined.

Most of the Special Forces guys pick up a call sign at some point in their service. Usually, it is one chosen for you. I had picked up the moniker, "The Hulk," while at Delta Force for two reasons, although the guys at Delta would say it was for three reasons. First, I was not hugely tall at six feet one inch; however, I must admit that I was built massively, which was not obvious when I was fully dressed. Secondly, for the most part, I was a mellow easygoing guy. However, when engaged in battle or a bar fight, I underwent a transformation, much like the Hulk in the TV program of the same name. The intensity I displayed when I fought was scary. It even scared me sometimes. However, it was inspirational to those that reported to me.

And finally, a falsehood perhaps, because, well, the ladies have told me on occasion, and I tended to agree with them, I thought of myself as a good-looking guy with dirty blonde hair down over my ears and light blue eyes, and a chiseled nose and full lips. However, the guys said I would turn green and ugly like the Hulk and just scare off the enemy. If you have ever seen Michelangelo's sculpture of David—yes, that one, except for his privates that look a bit small in proportion to the rest of his body, especially his hands—you would have a good picture of yours truly. Again, except for my privates.

The fall of the Soviet Union had given the Cuban government cause to look elsewhere for support and military supplies. The Chinese were more than willing to ally themselves with Cuba and, hopefully, create a base of operations just ninety miles from the United States. U.S. intelligence was concerned at this turn of events and had contracted the Sect-Intel Group to follow up on a covert operation they had started.

In spite of my heart condition, I felt fine and enjoyed my work immensely. The experiences I had while at Delta and later at the CIA and Department of Defense had been very rewarding for me. Working at Sect-Intel, while not the same as being with Delta or even the CIA, had been very gratifying... lots of field assignments, no one shooting at you, and best of all, no assigned desk for me at the main office. The only thing that had eluded me so far in my life was a love relationship. Don't get me wrong. I've had my share of lovemaking. But the fulfilling emotion of sharing real love that I long for was missing from my life at the moment. Come to think of it, I'd never had that emotion.

Alex had branded my team within Sect-Intel the Alpha Team. I think it was the love of his life, Julia, who was responsible for our name. In her business, the investment field, alpha was what you strived for. It was a measurement of how much you were exceeding the indices. So, the expectation for our team was always to be better that the average. I liked that. My slogan had always been "go for it," so it fit well with our team's name of Alpha.

As part of my team, Jackie Allison was working with Sect-Intel. She had formerly been a covert operative with the Drug Enforcement Administration, the DEA. Jackie had planted listening and camera devices in the three rooms of the Cuban officials who were staying at The Nikko Hotel in Mexico City, the same guys I had my eye on at the restaurant.

Jackie was in her early thirties, spoke three languages, had been trained as a flight engineer, and was a licensed pilot, checked out on various planes, including jets. Besides all her qualifications, she was a knockout with legs that would not quit, medically enhanced breasts, and long brown hair that caressed her sensuous neck and shoulders. Her dark eyes were warm and inviting as was her demeanor. Not that I was looking or anything. She was a natural for this operation, having been covertly embedded in various operations during her years with the DEA. Today, disguised as a maid, she had gained entry into the Cubans' rooms and planted micro listening and video devices throughout their rooms. The Chinese officials meeting with the Cubans at the San Angel Inn had flown into Mexico City that morning and were not staying in Mexico City. They would fly out immediately at the conclusion of the lunch meeting, and thus we would be unable to acquire any intelligence from them.

My wireless device rang in my ear. I gave it a touch

with my index finger to answer the call. "Yes," I answered.

"Father, I have sinned, and it's been thirty years since my last confession," Jackie's sultry voice carried into my earpiece.

"Well, my dear, this should be interesting," I replied.

"All set on my end," she said, softly laughing. "Do you still have eyes on them?"

"They seem to be wrapping things up here. I am going to change out of my Father Thomas disguise and follow the Cubans. Hopefully, they'll go to their hotel. With the amount of tequila they consumed here, they should be in no shape to do much more. From my observation, things went well. Lots of smiling and toasts after lunch," I said.

"Great. We're all set up at the Presidente Hotel, a few blocks from them. You and Joey are in Room 601, connecting to my and Melissa's room, which is 603. Joey has set up the video link to their rooms. We have two cameras in each room, and frankly that may give us more information than we need ... if you know what I mean,." she said.

The third member of my team, Joey, had joined us a year ago. Joey Valentine was born in Detroit, Michigan to an African-American mother on Valentine's Day. His birth certificate read "father unknown." His loving and protective mother and grandmother raised him. Joey showed an aptitude for computers at the age of twelve, and his mother

quickly exposed him to programming and writing code in the hope that would be his ticket out of the ghetto. Every day through high school, his mother would walk him to school and his grandmother would pick him up in the afternoons. Their efforts paid off when Joey graduated from high school and won a scholarship to Michigan State. He graduated from there in just three years with a master's degree in computer science. Something that was totally foreign to me -- computers and science, that is.
His future had been bright, and he told me that he had dreamed at one point of taking care of his mother and grandmother as soon as he entered the lucrative world of technology and Wall Street. His only mistake came weeks after graduating, when a local well-organized gang from his neighborhood threatened to kill his grandmother if he did not hack into a local bank and divert funds to a series of fraudulent accounts. Joey made the transfer successfully. However, the authorities tracking his breach were able to identify him. He was charged and found guilty. Appealing for mercy, his mother convinced the judge to place him on probation. The judge acquiesced and ordered probation for five years, after which his record would be expunged assuming no other infractions.

Joey was skinny as a rail, baby-faced, and five feet eight inches tall. He wore large black-rimmed trifocals and always dressed preppy. To me, he looked like a young scholar. This kid's smile was radiant and engaging, a sign of an outgoing personality and somewhat in contrast to the typical nerd. He loved these assignments. He thought he was a spy.

The fourth member of my team was Melissa Harrington, or as we called her, Mel. She was twenty-two years old, born in Tuskegee, Alabama. Mel had been tried as an adult for murder at the age of seventeen after she killed her stepfather. Her defense attorneys proved that her stepfather had physically abused her mother and had sexually molested Melissa from the age of fourteen years old. However, her attorneys were unable to prove that on the day she killed her tormentor, she had been acting in self-defense. I wished I had been there for her that day. I mean, I thought this young lady was special. She just got caught in a no-win situation. The case had been pleaded down to manslaughter, and she was found guilty. The judge reluctantly sentenced her to ten years in the Julia Tutwiler Prison for Women in Wetumpka, Alabama. Not a place I would want to be in. She never really talked about her time in prison. However, from what she did share, I could tell that she suffered more during her first year in prison than she had in four years at the hands of her stepfather. At least then she had her mother to console her. Learning Brazilian jujitsu, a martial arts technique designed for smaller persons and females, she vowed that she would never again be under someone else's control and she succeeded. At just over eighteen years old, she became the protector of many young women in her cellblock. Occasionally challenged by other inmates during her last three years, she was able to overcome these confrontations and was left alone for the balance of her sentence. Mel had developed a reputation as a badass, and it served her well. She taught the martial arts to others and received her high school diploma prior to her parole. Jackie and I were also well versed in the martial arts due to our own backgrounds, but Mel was having fun teaching Joey all about it.

She wore her black hair in spikes, cut very short around the sides. She was lean and muscular but not in a masculine way. At five feet six inches, with hazel bright eyes, well-balanced curvatures, and light skin, she was an attractive young lady. Internally, though, she was hardened, cynical, short-fused, and ready to strike at a moment's notice. We could tell that deep down, she was a kind, tender, loving person. Her past, however, made her mask those sentiments, as the demons inside her prevailed at times. I guess we all had our demons.

Replying to Jackie, I said, "Very well. I'll follow the Cubans to their hotel and then call you to let you know. I'll see you later."

I got up and walked towards the restaurant, leaving behind the courtyard, the fountain, and the smell of the horses. Really, it was vivid in my mind—I could literally smell them. I entered a beautiful covered-patio area before stepping into the restaurant that had quite a history, as another waiter who had also kept asking me every fifteen minutes if I needed something had told me. These guys could double up as tourist guides. He said the structure had originally been built as a monastery in the 1600s, and it remained pretty much the same over the years, becoming a hacienda and later a world-renowned restaurant.

I made my way to the front of the restaurant through a foyer while admiring the Mexican colonial architecture. I was on my way to the restroom where I would shed my Father Thomas disguise. Once there, I immediately became aware of the strong smell of disinfectant, but I also noticed that two small figures had followed me into the restroom. Walking towards the urinal, I pretended to use it while keeping a vigilant eye on the two men.

"Are you a priest?" asked one of the men in English. Both men were now behind me as I stood at the urinal, not giving me much space. I didn't like people invading my space, especially when I was supposed to be holding my piece—well, you know what I mean.

"Yes I am," I answered. "And I would appreciate it if you would stand back a little." Faking a Spanish accent for some idiotic reason, I turned my head and saw that both men were Chinese, or at least Asians. Immediately, the hairs on my neck went up, initiating a fight-or-flight response and increasing the levels of estrogen and testosterone in my system. Shit, I had not seen these men before. I assumed they were part of the Chinese officials group, and I hated myself for having missed these two in my original observation.

"You have been watching our group have lunch. Why?" demanded the Chinese guy on my immediate right, not moving an inch from behind me.

I began laughing as a means of distracting the two men while I planned my next moves. As the two Chinese men looked at each other, trying to figure out what the hell I was laughing about, I turned to my right and the Hulk in me unleashed a massive strike with my right elbow on the Chinese man's face to my right. Hearing his nose break and seeing the blood spatter on the white tile walls, I continued my motion to the right and, lowering my left shoulder, I scooped the second little man off the floor with my left hand grabbing him through his legs. With my right hand, I held onto the man's neck, raised him over my head and violently threw him against the wall. The first thing that hit the wall was the back of his head, rendering him unconscious. Mistakenly, the first Chinese man attempted to get up off the floor only to receive a quick kick in the jaw, his teeth biting off a piece of his tongue, and knocking him out. Blood was spattered all over the floor and walls of the small bathroom. Quickly washing my hands and face, I removed as much blood as possible. Turning my jacket inside out to reveal a khaki-colored blazer, I detached my religious collar from my black shirt and removed the white-haired wig I had been wearing. I took one last look in the mirror as I shook my dirty blonde hair, and with my left hand I reached for the door. Stepping out, I pressed the lock button from the inside, securing the bathroom, at least for a while, from anyone wishing to enter.

Walking out of the bathroom, I located the Cubans who were now saying their good-byes to the Chinese in front of the restaurant. I walked off in a different direction but remained close enough to pick up the trail of the Cubans as they walked away. I assumed that the two men in the bathroom would be discovered in a few minutes, and the Chinese officials would know someone had been watching them. Whether they would communicate that or not to the Cubans, I did not know. Protocol told me that they would. So I figured the Cubans would be alerted and would search for listening devices upon arrival in their rooms or be on the lookout for someone following them. I was still pumped from the action in the small bathroom.

The Cubans hailed a taxi in front of the restaurant, and I jumped into another taxi, a beat-up light blue Volkswagen Beetle, whose front passenger seat had been removed to accommodate a passenger in the back seat. I told the driver to follow the Cubans' taxi. Sitting back, I tried to calm down from the adrenaline rush I had just experienced. My heart was still pounding from the experience as I registered a slight uneven heartbeat.

"Americano?" asked the driver, who was massive in size and not very clean.

"Sí," I replied, not really wanting to get into small talk.

"¿Le gusto el restaurante?" asked the taxi driver. I guess he now assumed I spoke Spanish.

"Muy bueno," I replied, closing my eyes and covering my face with both hands while I caught my breath. *"Mucho tequila, duele cabeza."*

The taxi driver laughed, but got the point that I had a headache and he left me alone.

Dialing Jackie, I looked around the small cramped taxi to identify a foul odor. It stank from something – his lunch, him, or who knows what it was. As she answered, I said, "We may have to make alternate plans in order to listen"– pausing – "to your parents talk about our wedding." I did not want the taxi driver to pick up anything from our conversation.

"Understood," she said. "Where are you?"

"I think I am going to stop at the Presidente Hotel. Then I'll call you," I replied. "Where is your sister, Melissa?"

"She is on overwatch at the hotel lobby. She is doing great," she replied. "Are you all right? You sound a bit winded."

"Yeah, I'm fine. Too much tequila, maybe," I said, noticing the driver was looking at me through the rearview mirror. I looked at the driver and smiled.

"¿La Señorita?" asked the driver, as I disconnected the call.

"Sí. La Señorita," I replied, trying to cut the conversation short.

"You going to marry at the San Angel Inn?" asked the driver.

Fuck, this gordo guy was relentless. He just didn't stop talking.

"Yes. How long before we get to the hotel? You already lost my friends in the other taxi," I said, making an attempt to change the conversation and sounding a bit perturbed.

"Sorry, sir. I always say, if you are going to die and go to hell, you should come to die in Mexico City because it takes forever to get anywhere," said the driver, laughing.

"I'll keep that in mind," I responded, politely laughing with the driver and trying to calm down. Can anyone die from a bad smell?

CHAPTER TWO

New York City

In economics, reflexivity refers to the self-reinforcing effect of market sentiment, whereby rising prices attract buyers whose actions drive prices higher still until the process becomes unsustainable and the same process operates in reverse leading to a catastrophic collapse in prices.

—From Wikipedia

The last thing he said, sounding very much like Henry Kissinger in his calm, deep, and somber monotone was, “Keep buying until it reaches 45, and then call me.” He hung up the phone.

Nikolas Akakios, at age sixty, was listed in Forbes magazine as one of the top fifteen richest men in the world. He had made his fortune trading stocks, commodities, and currencies around the world. Born in Athens, Greece, he had learned the basics of trading as a young man helping his parents run a small local retail business catering to tourists. He observed diligently the reflexive nature of the consumers who would gather at a small open-air kiosk to buy jewelry while ignoring other similar kiosks. He summarized, at the age of 12, that buyers tended to follow others as sheep and emulate their reflexes. He made sure that hired would-be buyers always occupied his parent's little ten-by-ten-foot open-air kiosk, just as tourists would begin their descent on the local street market area. His hired buyers would create a buzz and later return the merchandise they had pretended to buy as the tourists left the area to return to their cruise ships with bags full of his father's junk.

Young Nikolas had begged and pleaded with his father to let him migrate to the United States and live with his uncle. Achill, his uncle, had written often to his father, and young Nikolas had intently absorbed the stories about America and its abundance of everything. The capitalistic system, his uncle would write, gave everyone who worked hard the opportunity to succeed and enrich themselves in a manner only dreamt of by many around the world. Nikolas had dreams - dreams of owning a car, a color television the size of a movie screen, and having money in his pocket to spend as he wished without worrying about paying the rent on the paltry little kiosk his father rented on a weekly basis. Yes, he had plans of his own and they did not include carrying on the family business, at least not in an open-air kiosk in Athens. No, not when the opportunities were so plentiful in America.

Finally, at the age of fifteen his father relented and arranged for Nikolas to join his Uncle Achill in New York.

Upon arriving in New York City, Nikolas began

attending high school and within weeks had landed a mailroom clerk's job at a local bank. His English was limited, but he more than made up for this through his discipline for work and perfect attendance. His entry into the banking and investment world had begun.

For twenty years he labored hard, always employed in a bank and later as a commodities trader. He learned his craft well and took advantage of his superior ability to grasp concepts involved in every step of his job. That led to his rapid ascension in the financial industry, a much quicker rise than others achieved. His determination, grit, and motivation did the rest. He ascended from mailroom clerk to manager of a branch for the bank. Then moved on and became an assistant for a commodities trading firm, then junior trader and finally, the head of the trading department.

Nikolas had always been grateful to his father for the trust he had shown in him and for allowing him to migrate to the United States. He had set up Akakios Trading as a side business and had made his father president in Athens and his Uncle Achill, vice president of the enterprise in New York. The business flourished with all types of imports and exports going back and forth between the United States and Greece. Nikolas kept tight reins on the business, serving as a consultant and advising when to pull back and when to take more risks as economic conditions warranted in his view. He had the uncanny ability to be three steps ahead in his thinking and could interpolate economic trends and their potential consequences as if he was doing simple math.

In his dark but well-appointed office on the top floor of the N.A. Limited office building in the center of the financial district in New York City, Nikolas ran his hedge fund and a multitude of other enterprises, including Akakios Trading, which he had taken over after the deaths of both his father and uncle. The view from his forty-fifth floor office was magnificent—the East River, the Hudson River, as well as Liberty Island and Governor's Island. Yet he kept the windows covered with drapes at all times. He had never gotten used to heights, and he had no interest in looking out on the expansive wide view of Manhattan offered by his location. The drapes were dark with red undertones that matched his imported area rugs from Istanbul. A constant malodorous odor emanated from the lack of natural light and the combination of the drapes and rugs. Dark brown leather chairs and sofas surrounded his ornate hand-carved wooden desk. Being on the top floor of the building, his office had a ceiling height of fifteen feet and was adorned with handmade red oak in the shape of a cupola running from end to end. The cupola's ceiling had been hand carved in the same four representations of a naked man in a chariot pulled by six incredibly beautiful horses, each following the next. The office gave one the feeling of sitting in a huge gazebo. This added warmness to the office, but at the same time, it darkened the room, providing some mysteriousness to the ambiance. Red oak bookcases lined the walls with a wide variety of reading material filling their shelves, from classics by Aristotle, Pythagoras, Machiavelli, Ralph Waldo Emerson, and Henry David Thoreau, to contemporary best sellers by Tom Clancy and John Grisham. He had read every single book that lined the shelves in his office. He was a voracious reader, but more than a reader, he was always a student. Nikolas kept himself in fairly good shape. It was hard with eighteen-hour days and eating most meals at restaurants. His demeanor and looks commanded respect. His salt-and-pepper hair, combed back, started about an inch from his full eyebrows. His deep blue eyes were penetrating, but his smile disarmed most men and attracted many women.

His phone rang. "Mr. Akakios, the stock reached 45," said the trader on the phone.

"Very well. What is our average price?" he asked.

"Sir, the average price is 41, and we now own one million shares even for a total cost of $41 million," the trader responded.

"Has the volume of purchases increased?" he asked, as he fixed the crease in his pants.

"In fact, the volume has tripled since we started buying

last week," the trader replied.

"Fine," he said. "Set a stop-sell order at 43 for the first 400 thousand shares and the balance at 42 and 41 for each 300 thousand tranche. Is the Dow Jones still up?"

"With about five minutes to go, the Dow is up 110 points, sir," said the trader.

"If we close over one hundred, buy $1 million worth of Nikkei call options, in the money for a short quick trade," he said as he sat back in his chair and removed his reading glasses. "Close the position if the options move ten percent either way. If you do it before midnight, call me and let me know. Otherwise, we'll talk first thing in the morning. Be ready tomorrow to start buying puts and calls in all the indices in both the U.S. and on the Nikkei."

He sat up in his chair and held the phone to his ear with his thick left hand. After hanging up with the trader, he clicked the phone with the index finger of his right hand and dialed his assistant. "Anna, what time is it in Beijing?" he asked.

"Mr. Akakios, it would be four in the morning now, sir," she replied.

"Very well, at six put a call in for Mr. Cong Wáng on the secure line. And Anna, if you have time, I'll take my tea now," he said, as he licked his lips and swallowed, almost tasting his afternoon cup of oolong tea that he loved so much.

"I have it ready for you, sir. I'll bring it in momentarily," she replied.

CHAPTER THREE

Shanghai, China

Director Chen Lee had awakened, as he did every day, at four in the morning to start his daily ritual of exercise and meditation. At forty-five years old, he had risen rapidly to lead the Ministry of State Security or MSS for the Peoples Republic of China or PRC. He was a short thin man whose icy dark eyes never looked directly at anyone but seemed to look right through them. With the bony little fingers of his right hand, stained yellow from nicotine, he reached over to turn off the alarm while still in the darkness that pervaded his bedroom. He immediately grabbed a Zippo silver lighter and proceeded to light his first cigarette of the morning... on the way to the four packs he would smoke that day. When he was twelve years old, his mother had become pregnant, violating China's law of one child per family. His father and mother had agreed to go through with the birth of their child and planned to arrange for her sister, who was married but unable to have children, to raise the toddler as if it was her own. Chen would have none of that, reporting his mother and father to the authorities and forcing the Lees to abort their unborn child.

The main objective of the MSS, it is believed, is to protect the interest of China's national security. Their methods have allegedly included corporate and government espionage by gaining commercial, technological, and military secrets by any means necessary.

Director Lee ran the MSS with a tight fist. He never traveled outside China and was distrustful of anyone around him. He thus was able to keep his double life secret. As Director Cong Wáng, he ran the Ministry of International Trade or MIT for the PRC. Cong Wáng was but a legend, and the MIT was simply a cover for international espionage, cyber warfare, and the vehicle he hoped would deliver the final blow to the United States after the initial punch in the gut it had sustained on September 11, 2001.

Operation Black Swan was his creation. In the making for two years, the plan was devised to bring down the United States economy, utilizing what had never occurred before, a flash crash of the markets. It would be a massive, rapid, one-day drop that would send fear into the hearts of many and create chaos in the dwindling capital system. He would seize upon the weakened state of the U.S. economy after the attack on the Twin Towers and the disruption of its economy as the "starter" for the fire he would bring to the United States. China was the nation's biggest banker, owning about twenty percent of the U.S. national debt, which stood at about $6 trillion at the start of this year. He knew that the events of 9/11 would require that the U.S.

would need to borrow more and more to lift its economy. His attack on the financial system would give China the upper hand; the PRC would become the Shylock, Shakespeare's fictional character, of the United States, thus assuring China's manipulation of its currency would go unabated for years to come without any intervention. Coupled with the goals of the cabal or the elite secret society, sometimes referred to as the "internationalists" that existed around the world, the old saying "the enemy of your enemy is your friend" was very prevalent in this unholy association.

"Director Wáng, good morning to you, sir," said Akakios, as Wáng picked up the phone, in his austere-looking office.

"Ah, Mr. Akakios, good to hear your voice. How are things this evening in the United States?" he asked.

"Good, Director. Things are looking good," replied Akakios.

"Tell me, sir, how do you see the U.S. stock market at this point?" he asked.

"Well, Director, I see the market recovering a bit more from last year's drop. The momentum seems to be there for a continued rise," Akakios responded.

"I see, I see. Good. We want the markets going up," he said, laughing, and added, with a slight cough, "The higher they go, the lower they can fall. Are you ready to execute on your end when I give you the word?"

Nervous, Akakios replied, "Yes, Director, we are ready. But we do need a heads-up a few days before you execute on your end."

"Of course. You'll have that. Are you taking care of my interests?" he asked.

"Yes, Director, you are all set, sir," Akakios replied.

"Mr. Akakios, it's gratifying to me to use America's own strength against them. The capitalistic system turned against itself. You are a valuable asset to the objectives of our group. I hope you are well rewarded," he said.

"Oh, I will be, sir. Trust me on that," Akakios responded, with a slight nervous laugh.

"Nikolas, I want you to put in some trades for us tomorrow before twelve noon Eastern Standard Time," the director said. "Sell our standard amount short market order on the following: retailer SuperStore, symbol SPER, SunMarc Bank, symbol SMBK, and lastly, electronics manufacturer Elo Teck, symbol ELTC. One million shares each. Understood?"

"Yes, sir," replied Akakios, repeating back the symbols.

"Onward then. We will converse again tomorrow and I will bring you up to date then. I will tell you when to close these orders. Have a good evening," he said.

"And you a good day, Director."

Director Lee sat back in his gray vinyl chair behind his

gray metal desk and looked around at his drab accommodations and dimly lighted office. It was inside a nondescript building, which was in a state of disrepair in the middle of Shanghai. No one would ever suspect this was the headquarters for the type of cyber warfare that was being conducted. Soon he would command the respect of the party leaders, and then his place in the hierarchy of the PRC would be awarded accordingly. He cared not about the amenities that came with being in a top leadership position; however, he craved the respect it would bring him amongst his peers. A quiet man of simple means, he had only one vice, his craving for young girls and boys to satisfy his pedophile lifestyle that he satiated five times a week.

CHAPTER FOUR

Varadero Beach, Cuba

It was early evening in Varadero Beach, one of the most beautiful beach resorts in the Caribbean. Located on the north coast of Cuba, about ninety miles east of Havana in the province of Matanzas, Cuba, Varadero is part of a peninsula that protrudes into the Atlantic Ocean, surrounded by crystal-clear blue-green waters. The sky had turned into a canvas of bright orange, with simmering yellow, light blue, and emerald green streaks above the horizon that changed ever so slowly as the sun receded into the majestic sea. It was quiet this evening; the breeze had subsided and the only sound one could hear was that of the gentle lapping of the waves caressing the shells on the beach. Back and forth, the rhythmic movement of the waves was gentle as the sea softly came into shore and retreated back unto itself. An occasional seagull would add to the natural sound of the beach as it searched for its evening banquet along the shoreline.

Colonel Abimbola Cruz sat on the second floor on the wide veranda that surrounded the entire first and second stories of the old wood cottage home. The home, built in the 1940s, had been restored to its original beauty and was painted white with azure blue trimmings throughout. This had been a reward from the Castro brothers in recognition of his allegiance and dedication to the revolution. He could smell the sweetness of the ocean along with the salt and brine, as he watched the glowing moon rise from the east over the Atlantic Ocean. As head of the Directorate of Intelligence for the Cuban government, he had risen rapidly in the Cuban military. He had achieved success in the year 2000 when he befriended Generals Naviles and Garces and foiled their attempt at the coup d'état of the Castro brothers. The generals, although slightly suspicious of the young man, had entrusted him with the assassination of twenty-one anti-Castro leaders in both Miami and Cuba, fourteen of whom had been successfully eliminated. The assassination of then-candidate George W. Bush had failed in Operation El Niño, but that would have been icing on the cake for the generals. More importantly, Operation Due Diligence in 2000 would have laundered billions of dollars by taking public, through a Wall Street stock offering, the private conglomerate of MonteCarlo Industries of Miami, Florida, a secretly held company of the Cuban government. The generals had planned on diverting the proceeds of the offering to their own personal accounts and depriving the Cuban government and the Castros of the funds.

Colonel Abimbola had not been privy to the generals' planned fraud. However, he felt responsible for not discovering the plan before the FBI, DEA, and CIA imploded the offering and had the SEC and DOJ take over MonteCarlo Industries confiscating the de facto assets of the Cuban government and the illicit riches accumulated over forty years.

Ricardo "Rick" Ramirez had been the CEO of MonteCarlo Industries, as well as head of the criminal empire in Miami that the Cuban government ran through him. Ramirez had been forcefully extracted by the CIA in 2000 while in Paris and had been flown to the United States to stand trial for racketeering, fraud, and drug smuggling. He was currently serving twenty years in a federal prison.

Colonel Abimbola was an imposing figure. Son of a mulatto Cuban father and an African mother, he was six feet four inches tall, with a shaved-head, and was black as night. Abimbola was the name of his maternal grandfather in Africa and meant, "born rich." He preferred to be called by his rank and first name to show off his African heritage of which he was very proud. Always in uniform, he stood a good six inches above his peers and the men that reported to him. He was feared by most. He had demonstrated his ruthlessness by executing many personally, with one shot to the head from his Ruger P45-caliber automatic pistol. This, he was proud to say, was following the examples of his mentors, the Castro brothers and Che Guevara, a leader of the revolution he had never met.

"So let's review the information we have so far,

Captain," said Abimbola, as he moved forward in his comfortable wicker chair on the open patio area of his home. He opened the file that had been brought in by Captain Ruiz.

"Yes, Colonel. It's been two long years putting all the pieces together, sir. However, I think we have a clear picture of the players that prevented us from carrying out Operation Due Diligence," said the captain as he displayed pictures contained in the file and placed them on the small wicker table between them.

"Who is this?" he asked, looking at the first picture.

"That is Alejandro Cardenas, an ex-CIA, non-official cover operative. Cardenas worked for the CIA after graduating from law school in Miami. He operated as an attorney with postings in Venezuela, Panama, Miami, and in other countries," said the captain, moving the photograph to one side. "We believe that Cardenas and his team extracted Ramirez from Paris in 2000. And while in custody, Ramirez was tortured to give up the names of the generals."

"Where is he now?" Abimbola asked, looking up from the picture to stare at the captain.

"He lives in Chicago, Illinois. He is owner and president of the Sect-Intel Group, a private security and intelligence company that is under contract to the U.S. government and other governments. They also contract to private and public companies. The main expertise of his firm is uncovering corporate espionage," replied the captain.

"Aha! He is in the spy craft industry. Just like us. You know, Captain, he at least took down the generals," he said with a dry laugh. Looking at the next picture, he remarked, "I know this beautiful lady. She is Julia Muller Estrada Palma, the newly elected president of the Cuban Council in Exile and one of the targets we missed in Operation Clean Sweep.

"Yes, sir, that is correct," responded the captain.

"Did you know that the first president of Cuba in the early 1900s was her great-great-grandfather?"

"It's in the file, Colonel."

"Why is she in the group? She was the investment banker who was leading the syndicate to take Rick Ramirez's MonteCarlo Industries public and was targeted for assassination," he asked.

"Well, Colonel, she was not directly involved in taking down Ramirez. As a matter of fact, she was our pawn in the laundering of those $10 billion. However, while not married, she lives with Cardenas. They met in the 1990s and enjoyed a six-year love affair while they were both still married," said the captain.

"I recall that the attempt on her life killed her husband and his mistress, instead of her. She owes us for that favor," he said, laughing. "I guess I know how to get to Cardenas now."

"Exactly," said the captain.

Picking up a third photograph from the file, Colonel Abimbola said, "Another beautiful lady. Who do we have here?"

"That, sir, is Jackie Allison. She was with the DEA, or Drug Enforcement Administration, and was covertly embedded in the Ramirez organization in Miami. As a matter of fact, she was Ramirez's lover. Ramirez has admitted to an asset we have in the United States that he mistakenly confided too much information to Allison. It was she, we believe, who came out and spilled the beans on Ramirez's drug smuggling operation and our Operation Due Diligence," he said. "One more point of interest, if I may, sir."

"Go ahead," he said. "But it looks like Ramirez was thinking with the wrong head. Idiota!"

"Allison, prior to joining Ramirez, had been covertly embedded in the Jimenez cartel in Mexico. She and her husband flew drugs for them. Her husband was killed in an accident when their plane crashed on one of their runs. All the cocaine aboard was lost to the fire, but $2 million in diamonds were never recovered," he added.

"Busy girl, this Allison. And where is she now?" he asked, sitting back in his chair as the wicker creaked. He looked straight into the captain's eyes.

"She left the employ of the DEA soon after the Ramirez trial. We lost her for a while. But now she has resurfaced at Sect-Intel Group, working for Cardenas," he replied.

"I wouldn't mind spending a few hours with Agent Jackie. How about you, Captain?"

"Yes, sir, that could be most enjoyable," replied the captain.

"Well, if we play our cards right, we will have a chance to do just that," he said, raising his eyebrows and sticking his very long tongue out. Laughing, he continued, "I will pull rank and be first, however."

"That's understood, Colonel," added the captain.

"So, we have all of our eggs in one basket. How convenient is that? Captain, you have done an excellent job. Congratulations," he said, as he sat back and crossed his legs. He looked at the seagulls silhouetted in the now grayish-orange sky, maneuvering over the shore against the backdrop of the rising moon. "Now we can plan to get even with these three and extract our payback. Stay a while and enjoy some rum and a good cigar from my private collection."

"By all means, Colonel. Thank you," said the captain.

CHAPTER FIVE

Chicago, Illinois

You know you're in love when you can't fall asleep because reality is finally better than your dreams.

—Dr. Seuss

Sect-Intel Group had its offices at the Garland Building in Chicago, a few steps from Michigan Avenue's Cultural Mile and overlooking Lake Michigan. After Alex and Julia narrowly escaped the assassination attempt in 2000, they spent three months together in Paris. Upon his return, Alex decided to abandon his work as a non-official cover operative or NOC with the CIA. However, having spent much of his life in the tradecraft business, he opted to continue in the same line of work, but this time as an owner of an intelligence and security company instead of as an operative. The many contacts and friendships he had developed through the years would prove very advantageous to him as he opened his new business. Alex's choice of an office building had been easy. Not only did he enjoy the proximity to Michigan Avenue and the incredible view of Lake Michigan, but the Garland Building was also home to Muller, Anderson and Associates, Julia's own investment banking firm.

His first marriage to his high school sweetheart, Alicia, had suffered irreparable damage. It had become a companionable relationship due to his continuous travels and the work-related stress associated with his covert operations in Latin America. He still carried the guilt that the fatal heart attack suffered by Alicia had been exacerbated by his relationship with Julia during his six-year affair with her in the 1990s.

Alex had been in Paris in 1990 on a covert assignment with the CIA to protect Julia. However, from the moment of their accidental encounter both Alex and Julia fell in love. Alex had looked at her and had seen immediately that Julia's demeanor was one of self-assurance. Her beauty, with her round penetrating blue eyes, sensuous lips, silky white skin, and long thick blonde hair, was vividly entrancing. They had found a love that soul mates are supposed to enjoy without limitations and encumbrances. Yet theirs was a sinful affair of joy, laughter, sensuous lovemaking, friendship, and trust...all wrapped in a precarious veil of infidelity. Now the soul mates were together, enjoying their reality after life's many turns. The love they had shared as sinful partners had rekindled itself after four years of separation and a traumatic experience in which Julia's husband, along with his mistress, had been killed in the attempt on Julia's life. Once again guilt had shrouded their lives, but they had learned to compartmentalize, perhaps selfishly, the events of their past. Alex had suffered watching Julia's marriage to her philandering husband and his lack of respect for her during those years. Yet he had admired her dedication to her marriage and her unwillingness to break up his during their long affair.

Fate had joined them twice and they would both relish every moment going forward as soul mates. For Alex, life was good. Together with Julia and in a new environment, he looked forward to spending the rest of his life next to her and developing his business. He was happy for a change, although phantoms from the past occasionally visited when least expected.

Julia had been a partner at Goldman Sachs in the 1990s and had been in Paris at the request of the La Sùreté Nationale, France's criminal police bureau, which had been the inspiration for the FBI in the U.S. and Scotland Yard in England. Manuel Noriega, president of the Republic of Panama, had been deposed and arrested by the United States in Operation Just Cause. Noriega had been an ally of the United States and a confidante of the CIA. However, in the late 1980s, he began selling U.S. secrets to the government of Cuba and increasing his many criminal activities related to drug dealing. These activities forced the hand of the U.S. to act against him. After his arrest, France also wanted Noriega for money laundering and other charges. Since Julia had had dealings with Noriega while she was at Goldman, she would be a key witness for La Sùreté's criminal investigation of him.

The United States Department of Justice, or DOJ, also wanted Julia as a witness and feared her life would be in danger in Paris from Noriega's goons or Cuban intelligence operatives who had a vested interest in protecting Noriega.

The DOJ's fears became a reality when four Spanish-speaking operatives attempted to kidnap Julia only to be thwarted by Alex and his CIA team. A limo occupied by Alex and Julia was headed northwest on Rue de Turbigo in an area known as Châtele-Les Halles, a tourist area and underground shopping mall during the day, but not the best place to be at night, when it was attacked. The result was four Spanish-speaking operatives, probably Panamanian or Cuban, lay dead in the streets of Paris. The traumatic event had cemented the relationship of the couple.

"Mr. C., Mrs. Muller is on her way to your office," said a voice over the intercom.

"Thank you, Joy," replied Alex, pressing down on the intercom button and getting up to greet Julia. His office was spacious but casual. It was like an inviting living room, with a soft green sofa lined with bright-colored cushions and comfortable chair where visitors could sit, discuss topics, and relax. He did not use the overhead lighting. Instead, he preferred to use the well-positioned lamps on the tables beside the sofa and chairs that added to the relaxed ambiance of the room. His desk which was positioned to one side of the room, was a twelve-foot-long table made of solid dark oak that doubled as a small conference table for more formal discussions.

Julia walked in with her radiant smile that made his heart skip a beat. "We are going to have to do something about that last name," he said as he inhaled a whiff of her perfume. He loved the scent so much; it always gave him a flashback to their first encounter in Paris twelve years earlier.

"Well, it's up to you. At the moment it's the one I've got," she replied, still smiling.

"This package came in for you. I was going to take it home, but since you are here, I may as well give it to you now," he said, picking up a small brown box from his desk and at the same time pressing the intercom button twice.

"Why did they not deliver it to my office?" she asked.

"Well, it's for you, but it's addressed to me," he responded.

"You bought me something from Amazon?" she asked, a bit perplexed. As she began opening the Amazon box, Alex's office was filling up with his associates.

"What's going on?" she inquired nervously.

"Just open it," he said with a wide smile. He winked at Andy Anderson, Julia's partner, who had walked in with an entourage from their investment-banking firm that was located just two stories above Alex's office.

"What are you people doing here?" she said, removing the filling from the box and seeing a small jewelry box.

Alex could see her anticipation and feel her excitement as she fumbled to open the case. He saw her eyes widen as she pulled out a three-carat diamond ring. Alex nodded to Andy and a champagne cork startled everyone in the room.

"You bought me a diamond ring from Amazon? Really?" she asked.

With everyone laughing, Alex replied, "Well, it was that or e-Bay. I had a credit in both accounts."

"Very funny. I love it. I don't care where it's from. Don't anyone start drinking. I haven't heard the question yet," she said, looking around the room.

Alex moved close to Julia. He knelt before her and looked up into her blue and now misty eyes and said, "Julia, will you marry me?"

"You bet, you S.O.B.," she replied as Alex got up. Wearing the biggest smile ever seen on him, he embraced her.

Everyone cheered as Andy began filling the champagne glasses. They all enjoyed the moment. Julia and Alex had always had a certain effect on people near them. Their happiness when together exuded love that permeated everyone around them. The party lasted for a few more minutes as they drank all the champagne that Andy had brought down, and then everyone began to go back to their respective offices.

"Joy, thank you for arranging this surprise. We are going to take off and go home," said Alex to his assistant.

"My pleasure. It was lots of fun," said Joy. "Congratulations, Mrs. C.-to-be."

"Oh, thank you, Joy. Please, I've asked you to call me Julia," she said.

As they walked out of the office, Julia remarked, "Really? Amazon?"

"No, not Amazon nor e-Bay. I hope you like it," he replied, looking into her eyes again.

"I love it and I love you," she said, embracing him as they entered the elevator.

Alejandro Cardenas. Alex, as most everyone knew him, had arrived in Miami at six years of age when his parents had immigrated to the United States fleeing the newly formed Communist government of Fidel Castro in Cuba. The Cardenas family had assimilated well to their new country. They learned the language, found jobs, and went about their lives with comfort and tranquility. Alex attended the local high school, enrolled at the University of Florida, where he earned a bachelor's degree in business, and later graduated with a law degree from the University of Miami. During his studies at the University of Miami, he was recruited by the CIA with the promise that he would be involved in the overthrow of Fidel Castro's Communist regime. He had distinguished himself in international law studies and had spoken in public forums against the oppression of socialist dictatorships in Latin America. Alex had become an American citizen while in high school and he had developed a love for his new country. Yet, he could not help but feel a calling to be part of a mission to liberate Cuba... a country that his parents had been forced to leave... abandoning everything behind to assure freedom and safety for themselves and their son. Alex saw his role with the CIA as a way he could both serve his new country and help to liberate his country of birth. The liberation of Cuba had not come to fruition during his tenure with the CIA. However, he was satisfied that he had served his country. The training, contacts, and experiences he had would be invaluable in his new endeavor.

At six foot two, he was tall, and his mother, Carla, was always kidding that he took after his American Uncle Peter who had married her sister in Havana. This would always lead his father, José, to retort, "That's not funny, Carla." Alex never knew that it was Uncle Peter, himself a CIA agent working in the American Embassy in Havana during the '50s, who had recommended him for recruitment to the CIA.

As Alex and Julia exited the elevator on the lobby floor,

the aroma of the freshly brewed coffee captivated their sense of smell. They headed to the small coffee shop and asked the barista for a macchiato, the closest thing to a Cuban cortadito- hot steamed milk with a double espresso and sugar, lots of sugar. This had become their daily ritual as they left the office.

"So, how was your day?" she asked.

"Busy as usual," he said as they headed to the underground parking lot. "I've got the Alpha Team in Mexico City. They are following up on a case we picked up from the CIA last week.

"I'll tell you more later, but I have to go to Mexico City myself soon," she said. "What else is going on?"

"You'll like this one. You know who Nikolas Akakios is?" he asked as they entered their car.

"Who doesn't?" she replied.

"Well, my new client, an electronics manufacturer, thinks that someone in his company is sharing confidential information with one of Akakios's companies that is a competitor. Not only is he using the information to underbid my client, but he is also using it as insider trading knowledge to benefit from their stock volatility," he explained. He looked both ways before exiting the parking garage, making a right turn at North Wabash Avenue and then another quick left onto Washington Street.

"Clever. He buys the stock on the anticipation of a

government contract before it is reported in the news and then underbids the contract, but not before selling the stock short before it drops. Quite the stock trader savant he advertises himself to be," she summarized.

"It is quite the scheme, isn't it?" he asked rhetorically. "I'm getting involved personally on this one. I'm going to enjoy it. So, what's up in Mexico?"

"Potential merger and acquisition. My clients are looking to acquire a Mexican filmmaker and distributor. Their feeling is the Spanish population in the U.S. is growing dramatically and they want to add to their capabilities in that sector," she replied.

"Makes a lot of sense. When do you go?" he asked, as he made the turn onto North Michigan Avenue that would take them to their condominium.

"Don't know yet, but soon," she replied.

"I don't know if you should go there alone," he said. "I mean, when I go, I have a bulletproof SUV and three armed bodyguards."

"You make it sound like the Old Wild West," she said. "Is it that bad there now?

"No, I don't mean it like that. But it depends on where you go and how you dress. What is known as Greater Mexico City has a population of almost twenty million. That's a lot of people for one city. All kinds of things can happen. Kidnapping is a big business," he said. "I would feel better if you have someone with you. One of my guys, for instance."

"No problem. Just make sure he is cute," she said.

"I'll make sure. You want to stop for a Thai dinner?" he asked.

"No. I have a better idea. Let's go home and celebrate. I have a new scanty white lace Victoria's Secret ensemble I put away for this occasion," she said.

His eyes opened wide as he looked at her with a mischievous smile. "Let's," he said. He grabbed her left hand tightly with his right and stepped on the accelerator of his sleek black Porsche 911 GT2 Turbo with its natural brown leather interior, maneuvering the gearshift while still holding her hand.

CHAPTER SIX

New York City

Santería, also known as Regla de Ochá or La Regla de Lucumí, is a syncretic religion of Caribbean origin, which developed in the Spanish Empire among West African slaves. Santería is influenced by and syncretized with Roman Catholicism. Its liturgical language, a dialect of Yoruba, is also known as Lucumí.

—From Wikipedia.

Marta Oliva had secretly become Nikolas Akakios's most influential counselor. Originally a maid in his home, she had ascended to a position of trust in the Akakios's hierarchy. Marta was a *Santera* or priestess in the Santeria religion and had inducted Akakios into that religion many years ago.

Marta, an Afro-Cuban, had arrived in Miami during the Mariel boatlift in 1980. Castro had taken advantage of then-president Jimmy Carter's preoccupation with the Iran hostage crisis to empty his prisons of criminals, malcontents, the sick, homosexuals, and anyone else he wanted to get rid of. He had opened the gates to a mass exodus of over one hundred thousand Cubans who arrived in Miami by boats between April and October of that year. Embarrassed by this uncontrolled influx, the United States was able to negotiate an end to this exodus but not before Castro had achieved his desired goal.

Having been relocated to New York, Marta, at age twenty-two, ended up working as a maid in the home of Akakios. In a matter of weeks she seduced him after just a handful of attempts. While the rest of the domestic staff would take weekends off, Marta would stay alone with Akakios in his luxurious apartment in Central Park West in New York City. She did not plan on being a maid for long. He would be her ticket to the finer things her new country had to offer.

When Marta joined Akakios, he was forty-two and single by choice. She soon found out that he had never seriously considered a wife, as he had no time to be fully engaged with what he considered a trivial pursuit. He was listed in local social magazines as one of the most desired bachelors in the city. Page Six of the New York Post chronicled his every move on a weekly basis. Yet he remained aloof at the idea of taking on a permanent wife. His ritual on Saturdays and Sundays as he woke up to the scent of freshly brewed tea, was to have in his room a breakfast consisting of two hard-boiled eggs, his oolong tea, and unbuttered toast. Marta would serve his breakfast and bring him the Financial Times and Barron's. Their conversation was limited. For one reason he seldom engaged in a long conversation with the help, and secondly, her command of the English language was very weak despite her studies in the evening to learn the language.

She noticed that Akakios would look at her as she served his breakfast, and his eyes would linger on her large firm natural breasts and then would follow her as she exited his room by lowering his gaze to her well-rounded, sculptured, and protruding derriere.

After three weeks of this ritual during which she tempted Akakios weekly with a lower cleavage on her maid's blouse, she made a bold move. Having served his breakfast tray along with the newspapers on a table beside his bed, she stood next to Akakios, and while he was surreptitiously looking at her breasts, she removed her *eleke* bead necklace and slowly began unbuttoning her white blouse. With a coquettish smile, she looked straight into Akakios's eyes. She had made it a point not to wear a bra, and as she unbuttoned her last button, she could see his eyes widen and his puffy eyebrows rise as her exposed breasts and hardened nipples captivated him.

"¿Sí?" she asked simply, flashing a wide smile with pearl-white teeth while still looking into his eyes.

"Sí," he responded with a small sigh as he removed the light green silk sheet covering him in an invitation for her to join him in bed.

"Wait a little," she said as she began unzipping her

white skirt from behind and slipping it off in a rhythmic dance to expose to him her well-groomed front without any panties.

Looking at his erection under his dark blue silk pajamas, she said, “No hurry, please.” She climbed in bed, and kneeling and straddling him with her masterpiece over his face, she began working on his manhood, now fully erect, with her hands and her full lips.

“I want *nalgadas*. You know what is?” she asked.

Akakios could hardly speak. He was in a trance. Finally, he said, “No, I don’t know.”

She let go of his throbbing manhood with her right hand and began spanking herself in her right cheek right over his face. “Like that, hard. You do,” she said, almost demanding.

He followed her commanding words, first with his right hand, and then his left as she lowered her rear onto his face and mouth, so that he could partake in satisfying her. After a few minutes, he made an effort to turn her around so that he could penetrate and enjoy her warmth, but she resisted.

“No! Today this only,” she said, as she stroked him faster and harder and utilized her full lips for maximum effect.

He went at her faster and deeper, trying to keep pace with her, but he finally succumbed to her erotic undertaking and stretched back fully... allowing nature to take its course.

Marta sat in bed next to him and retrieved her bead necklace with her right hand from the night table. She made the sign of the cross holding onto the necklace, and replaced it around her neck. She picked up her blouse and skirt and, without saying a word, walked naked out of his room.

She had undergone the full ritual of *Santería* in Cuba at the age of sixteen. It was estimated that four million people practiced the religion, with about seventy-five percent of them in Cuba, about twenty thousand in the United States, and the rest in countries around the Caribbean and in Latin America. Originating in West Africa during the Spanish Empire, the religion had spread to the Caribbean, as tribal kings, politicians, and community leaders were enslaved and transported to the New World. The newly arrived slaves were baptized and forced to accept the Catholic religion and thus they hid their beliefs and deity within the Roman Catholic saints and practices.

Not having a central creed, *Santería* was a system of religious customs using trance and divination in order to communicate with ancestors and deities. These customs encompassed animal sacrifice, sacred drumming, and dance.

Marta had received her *eleke* necklace as the first step in the ritual of her initiation into becoming a Santera or priestess. The colors and shapes of the eleke-beaded necklace were chosen after the *orichiá* or saint was selected as the guardian of the newly initiated. The necklace was first bathed in a mixture of herbs, sacrificial blood, and other substances chosen by the *padrino* or godparent of the initiated. It was never to be worn during a woman's menstruation, sexual intercourse, or while bathing.

Marta's second step in the weeklong ritual was the creation of an image of the *orichiá* or *Eleguá*. After a consultation with a *Santero*, the image to be sculpted was chosen, and Marta was to keep this sculpture in her home to protect against evil spirits. Her third step was "receiving the warriors." These were items given to Marta by her *padrino*. They represented other saints she was to keep in order that they might dedicate their energies to protecting and providing her, as the newly initiated, on her new path. The final ritual that Marta performed was known as *Asiento* or "ascending to the throne." This was the most secretive and important step before the novice became "born again" into the faith. It was a process of purification. Upon completion, the aspirant, after a year's wait, became a *Santero* or *Santera* and could perform cleansings, provide remedies, and initiate others into the religion.

Marta would begin the process of initiating Akakios into her religion soon. She would take him through the first three steps of the ritual but never allow him to "ascend to the throne," the final ritual, and thus would keep her power over him. For a twenty-two-year-old immigrant, she was masterful, cunning, and goal-oriented. It seemed her orichiás were guiding her well.

Akakios lay in bed, still in a trance. He had never experienced the exaltation with another woman that he had felt with Marta. Nor had he given into a woman being the boss when in bed. She had left him exhausted but wanting more, much more.

CHAPTER SEVEN

Mexico City

Jackie had waited for an hour in the expansive and modern-looking lobby of the Hotel Nikko. With its white marble floors and stonewalls. The lobby was a pleasant place to wait with its white marble floors and stonewalls. It was adorned with natural plants and freshly cut aromatic flowers. A normal commuting time between the San Angel Inn and the hotel would have been twenty minutes or less. In Mexico City, a twenty-minute ride through the heavily congested streets could easily take one hour or more depending on the time of day. The Hotel Nikko, located on Arquimedes Avenue, a few steps from the main thoroughfare of Paseo de la Reforma, was a favorite of international and business travelers.

Jackie recognized the main official from a picture I had sent her from my phone a few hours earlier. I had taken it during my surveillance at the restaurant as the officials had walked into the lobby. She immediately called me, still stuck in traffic in Paseo de la Reforma, and told me to go directly to our hotel, not the Nikko, and get ready to listen. At the moment, there was not much I could do. It was all her show for now.

She had to make a move and plant listening devices on them, or at least on the main subject quickly for fear they would be warned or perhaps already had been by the Chinese after the occurrence at the restaurant. Jackie had intended to dress in sexy, inviting clothing but decided not to as she might be escorted out of the hotel by the staff thinking she looked like a prostitute or a call girl. Instead, she opted for business attire, a gray suit over her white silk blouse, a bright blue scarf around her neck.

The three Cubans walked or maybe staggered slowly into the lobby. They had removed their ties, loosened their collars, and carried their jackets over their arms. Not drunk, but definitely buzzed from the Agave Dos Mil Reposado Tequila Grand Reserve, a forty percent alcohol-content tequila they had drunk at the San Angel Inn.

Jackie pretended to look down at her phone and bumped into the main official, a middle-aged man named Arturo. As she faked falling, she grabbed onto him and brought him down with her on the marble floors. As she did, she placed a micro listening device on his jacket's top outside pocket. The two other men rushed towards them, extending helping hands as Jackie and Arturo made an effort to get up as inconspicuously as possible from the floor. Jackie was so close she could smell the tequila on the official's breath. She placed a second device on another Cuban official, inside the interior pocket of his jacket.

"Señorita, perdon. ¿Esta bien?" said Arturo.

"Yes," she said in English. "And you?" she replied,

brushing her left elbow with her right hand.

"I, I, good. Thank you," replied Arturo.

"Mexican?" she asked, looking at Arturo first, but including all three at the same time.

"No, Cubanos," said the third man, who had helped Arturo off the floor.

"Me gusta Cubano," she said, looking around, but returning her gaze to Arturo.

"¿Sí? ¿Porque?" asked Arturo.

Pretending to be embarrassed, she moved closer to Arturo and softly spoke into his right ear. *"Me gusta porque como estan..."* She hesitated, before adding, "hung. *No se como dice 'hung' en Español."*

"Hung?" he repeated with an inquisitive look. He turned to his other friends and asked, *"¿Que cosa es 'hung' en ingles?"*

"Colgar," said one of them.

"Coño, que cosa mas grande la Americana esta," said Arturo, as his eyes widened looking at her.

"Yes. The way Cubans are hung," she said, smiling back, licking her lips and rolling her eyes upward.

"You want drink? Bar?" Arturo said, attempting his best English.

"Yes. Margarita," she replied.

"Ah, I am Arturo, Margarita," he said.

"No, I am, *yo soy*, Angie. I want, *quiero*, margarita,"

she said, laughing at his confusion.

"*Váyanse para el carajo, que me voy a tomar un margarita con Angie*," he told his two companions.

"*Sí,* go to hell, I am drinking with Angie a margarita," she said, repeating what Arturo had said and smiling at the other two men.

Jackie and Arturo walked into the Japanese hotel lobby bar, called Yamashito, for margaritas... giving me time to get ready to listen to the conversation of these men. All team members were now wearing their COM devices and thus were able to listen to each other's conversations. She had been able to plant bugs in only two of the three. Hopefully, that would be enough.

I finally made it to the Hotel Presidente after my car ride. I could not get rid of the pungent smell from the taxi, and it made me think that everyone was looking at me because of it. What was that? Rotten mangos, a dead burrito, or worse?

I walked into Room 601, which I was sharing with Joey. "Are you all set?" I said.

"I'm all set. We have eyes and ears in the room. Plus Jackie bugged two of the guys. One stayed with her for drinks at the bar, and the others should be coming up to their rooms," Joey replied.

"Let's hope the Chinese did not tip these guys off and they don't go looking for bugs."

"Why? What happened?"

"Little bit of an encounter with two Chinese in the bathroom," I said.

"In the bathroom?" Joey repeated.

"Yeah, I like to piss in peace," I said, sitting down next to Joey and paying attention to the monitors that he had set up.

"Shit, I'll have to remember that," Joey said, opening his eyes wide.

"You better, and lift the seat when it's your turn," I said, laughing and jokingly rubbing Joey's head. "What do we have here?"

"These guys are pretty smashed. I don't know how much we'll get. Each is in his room. I have a feeling it's time for a nap. We'll have to see if Jackie can pull something out of the third and main guy."

"I don't know if 'pull something out' is what Jackie wants to do," I said, getting up and heading to my bed. I was still fighting a headache.

"Oh, shit. I didn't mean it that way."

"I know, kid. Just giving you a hard time," I said, lying down. "Let me know if something is going on. Let's listen to Jackie and the third guy; turn up the volume."

After a few minutes of listening to Jackie and the Cuban, I realized that there was nothing of interest going on with the conversation. All Arturo, the Cuban, wanted to do was get in Jackie's pants, and the more he drank the less they were going to get.

I called Jackie on her cell phone instead of using our COM system. As she answered, I said, "Listen, this guy is not going to give anything up. Cut him loose, and let him go back to his room before you have to carry him.

"OK, love. No, I didn't forget about our date. I'll be there in a few minutes," she replied, faking her response to me. Jackie clicked off her phone and faced her companion. We all continued to listen to their conversation.

"Listen, my darling Arturo, I have a previous engagement. I'm afraid I have to go," she said.

"I thought we were on a date," Arturo said, somewhat annoyed as he saw the opportunity to take her to his room evaporating.

"I know, and I'm sorry. I forgot I met this man earlier, and we made plans. Tell you what, I'll call you later, and maybe I can come up to your room," she said, taking a last sip from her margarita as she licked the salt from her glass and gathered her purse from the top of the bar.

"*Bueno, linda,* I was going to do things to you that you would not forget, *especialidades Cubanas, mi amor*," Arturo said, as he waved to the bartender and motioned for the tab.

"Oh my, Cuban specialties. I can't wait. I will definitely call you. What is your room number?" she asked, knowing full well what his room number was.

"Seventeen, zero, zero," he said, trying to stand up from the barstool.

She reached over and kissed him on the cheek. "Don't start without me. I'll call you later." With that, she grabbed her purse and walked out of the bar and out of the hotel, leaving Arturo with great anticipation and an arousal he was trying to conceal with his jacket.

As she walked out, she spoke through the COM system. "OK, I am out and on my way back to you guys. Anything from the other two?"

"*Nada, linda*. They are slouched in their beds recovering from their margaritas. Arturo, your boyfriend, is the boss. If we are going to get something, it will be from him. Sorry, you are not going to be treated to the Cuban specialties," I said, looking at Joey and opening my eyes wide.

"You forget I hung with Rick Ramirez for a while. I know about those Cuban lovers. I know a lot," she replied.

"Interesting verb you chose there, Angie," I said.

Joey looked at me with a wide grin and popping eyes, as I continued, "Well, you'll have to share with us Americanos—can't have any secrets in our team."

"Not a chance, boys, not a chance," she said.

Melissa, who had been on overwatch keeping an eye on Jackie, piped in. "Hey, I'm listening to all this, too, you know."

"Hey, Melissa, we share a room. I'll brief you later. You definitely need to know about these specialties," Jackie said. "Head back to the Hotel Presidente. We are done at the Nikko."

CHAPTER EIGHT

Shanghai, China

Director Lee walked down two flights of stairs into an office marked “Online Sales” on the front door. As he walked in and looked at the sprawling large open room, all twenty young computer hackers sitting behind workstations with double monitors got up and stood. The room smelled like it was sanitized daily, not a spec of dust anywhere. “Good morning,” he said, not looking at anyone in particular.

All twenty responded in unison, “Good morning, Mr. Director.”

“You can sit. I want to see those working on the following: SuperStore, SunMarc Bank, and Elo Teck. Come to the conference room now,” he said in a commanding voice.

Immediately, three young men, no older than twenty-two, stood up and followed Director Lee to a small private conference room within the large room. It consisted of a metal table and six metal chairs, and nothing else except for a picture of Chairman Mao that hung from a wall.

Director Lee pulled back a chair and sat down at the head of the table as the three young men waited to be told to sit down.

“Sit down. Who is working on SuperStore?” he asked,

looking down at his file.

"I am, Director Lee," said one of the men.

"Status?" he asked, still looking down.

"I am ready, sir. I have successfully entered their firewall and can retrieve at will all records of their customers, credit card information, debit card information, passwords, account numbers, and history of purchases at the store, sir," said the man, not looking directly at him.

"Will they know if we breach their security?" he asked without looking at the man.

"They won't at first, unless we want them to know. Otherwise, they will realize a breach within twenty-four hours, sir," replied the man.

"SunMarc Bank. Same questions," he said, lighting a cigarette.

"Yes, sir. I am also ready. I can retrieve all customer information, balances in all accounts, and credit card and debit card numbers issued by the bank. Home addresses, Social Security numbers, and any other information that is available for every customer of the bank, sir," said the second man, without looking at the director.

"Very well," Director Lee said, as he flicked some ashes into an ashtray. "Go on."

"The bank, because of its security, will know immediately that they have been breached, but not before we retrieve all the records, sir," the second man continued.

"This is good," Director Lee said, stubbing out the cigarette in the ashtray. "Next, Elo Teck."

"Yes, sir. I can retrieve at will all the specs on both Drone1 and Drone2, their experimental designs, and final manufacturing plans. I can also retrieve the company's signed contract with the U.S. Department of Defense for both drones. Elo Teck will know that it has been breached, but, again, only after we are in possession of the documents, sir," said the third man.

"You have done a good job," Director Lee said, looking over their heads as he took another cigarette from his pack. "Be ready to pull the trigger, all three of you, when I tell you. Understood?"

Looking down at the table, they all responded in unison, "Yes, sir. Thank you, sir." They waited for Director Lee to stand and then followed him out of the conference room to return to their workstations.

Director Lee stood by the door and looked at the derrieres of the three young men, taking a big drag from his cigarette before walking out.

He ran the Online Sales unit that had nothing to do with sales, but everything to do with hacking the systems of other governments and corporations. From these, the unit could steal plans, copy them, and manufacture the upcoming inventions. He was proud of his young team of hackers. They had breached many systems throughout the world. His most famous breach was about to happen, and once completed, it would mean a devastation of the United States economic system, comparable to nothing that had ever occurred. He took out another cigarette from the pack looking at his yellow-stained bony little fingers, and smiled as he walked up the two flights of stairs to his austere, gray office. Upon arriving there, he sat down behind his desk, picked up the phone and dialed his superior, General Dang Wu.

"General Wu, this is Director Lee," he said, speaking softly into the phone.

"Yes, Director. Go ahead," General Wu replied.

"General, you'll be happy to hear that the breach of Elo Teck has been successful. The technology that the company has developed is incredible, and we have every detail of the engineering and manufacturing plans.

"Tell me, Director," Wu said.

"What Elo Teck is calling Drone1 is a mother drone. It can either be deployed from the ground, a plane, or a helicopter. Once deployed, Drone1 can carry in its belly as many as ten of what is called the Drone2 or code name 'Flybees,' " he said, looking at his file and paraphrasing as he read the intelligence report. "These 'Flybees' are a little larger than a fly, but no bigger than a bee. You've heard the saying, 'I'd like to be a fly on the wall'?"

"Yes, of course, I have," Wu, replied.

"Well, General, the 'Flybees' are going to give the Americans the capability of inserting these micro drones anywhere a fly or a bee can fly. Micro drones with both eyes and ears. Imagine a room being swept for bugs prior to a meeting and then having the capability of flying one of these things into the room. Or inserting one into a car when there is a private conversation going on. The capabilities are limited only by the imagination," Director Lee said excitedly, raising his thin eyebrows.

"Well done, Director. I guess we also have the capability now, don't we?" Wu asked rhetorically.

"We will. Yes, of course," he replied.

"Then, Director, keep me posted as to the other items on the agenda. We are looking forward to the big day."

"I shall, General," he said as he waited for the general to hang up first.

CHAPTER NINE

Mexico City

It was six in the morning in Mexico City when I heard a phone ring and jumped from my bed. Both Joey and I had taken turns monitoring the Cuban officials' rooms throughout the night. There had been no activity whatsoever, except in relation to the main official, Arturo, who spent a few hours expecting a visit to his room from Jackie, or as he knew her, Angie. He finally decided to take matters into his own hands, so to speak, and fell asleep soon thereafter.

I made an effort to locate the sound of the ringing as I groggily got out of bed. Realizing it was coming from the monitors, Arturo's room to be specific, I made my way to a chair in front of the screens, banging into some furniture and waking up Joey.

"What's up, John?" asked Joey.

"Finally something may be happening, kid. This guy is getting a call on a sat phone," I replied, rubbing my two-day-old beard up and down with both hands "Joey, you mind brewing some coffee in that Mr. Coffee on the dresser? And by the way, knock on the door of the ladies' room. We need Jackie here to translate."

"*No problema, señor.* I need some coffee myself to wake up," he replied.

Getting up from the chair without taking my eyes from the monitor, I slipped on some jeans over my underwear.

Jackie walked in wearing a robe, as Melissa, dressed in a long shirt, trailed after her.

"Uh, that coffee smells good," said Jackie. "You got enough for all of us?"

"I started a brew for us," said Melissa. "Those pots only hold two cups."

Jackie was taking notes as she heard Arturo, the Cuban, talking to someone who appeared to be his superior from the tone of the conversation. "We are taping this, correct?" she asked.

"You bet, *Señorita*," said Joey.

"What is your boyfriend saying?" I asked, taking some powdered creamer and mixing it with the coffee that Joey had poured into a plastic cup.

"Wow! Lots of stuff going on here. We need to call Alex immediately after this call," she said.

My eyebrows shot up as she said that. "What is going on?" I asked impatiently.

"*Un momento, Señor*," said Jackie, looking at Melissa who had brought in some coffee for her. "Thank you, Mel. Men are so impatient."

After a few minutes, the conversation between Arturo and his superior wrapped up. Arturo began undressing on his way to the bathroom.

"Your boyfriend is doing a strip show, if you want to keep watching," I said, smiling and looking at Jackie.

"No, thank you. It looks like I didn't miss much," she said, looking at Melissa. "Turn that off or something. We need to call Alex so you can all hear what's going on."

Joey darkened the images on the monitors as all three of the Cuban men were going about their business.

"John, you want to call Alex?" Jackie asked.

"No. Go ahead and call him yourself. We have no protocol to follow here. Besides, I only picked up a few things myself. Go for it."

"Here, I have Alex on the line," said Joey, handing over their own sat phone to Jackie.

"Alex, good morning," said Jackie, as Alex responded with the same greeting. Jackie went on, "Alex, you'll want to take notes. We'll come back with the full tape, both audio and video, but I think you need to act now when you hear this."

"Go on, Jackie," Alex said.

"China has a cargo ship, the Da Dan Xia, which has left the port of Shanghai. Its destination: the Port of Lázaro Cárdenas, here in Mexico. Estimated travel time left is about four or five days, depending on the seas. Anyway, this ship has containers, fifteen to be exact, that are to be unloaded onto a Cuban cargo ship prior to reaching the port. The cargo ship will rendezvous with the Da Dan Xian in international waters, just west of the port," Jackie said, as she looked at her notes. "You got me so far?"

"Go ahead," said Alex.

"The cargo is destined for the FARC, the Fuerzas Armadas Revolucionarias de Colombia. Once the cargo is transferred, the Cuban cargo ship is to deliver the goods to the port of Cristobal Colon in Venezuela. After that, the Venezuelans in turn, will deliver the contents of the cargo to the FARC.

"So, the Revolutionary Armed Forces of Colombia, known as FARC, is getting a delivery from China via a Cuban ship making port in Venezuela at the Cristobal Colon port," Alex said. "So far, there is nothing wrong. What's on board for FARC? Did you get that? 'Cause if it's rice, we just wasted a lot of time."

"What if it is rice and beans? No, no, Alex. I am going to make your day, Boss. How about 150 tons of explosives, three million detonators, 150 projectile heads, and three thousand artillery shells?" she asked. "A little harder to digest than rice and beans, wouldn't you say?"

"That's huge," Alex said.

John, Joey, and Mel kept looking at each other in amazement as they listened to Jackie relate the conversation to Alex.

"There is more, Alex," said Jackie, as she pointed to her empty cup and motioned for someone to get her more coffee. Joey got up to refill her cup.

"The bill of lading is going to show that China sold the military supplies to Cuba, obviously. The ship needs to go through the Panama Canal. However, as soon as it does, it will be making a right turn to Venezuela, instead of heading to Cuba," she said as she made a face showing her disgust after sipping the now ice-cold coffee. "Mierda," she whispered to John.

"What's that?" asked Alex.

"No, that was not meant for you, Alex. Let me go on," she said. "This is very important. At the request of China, Cuba has agreed to infiltrate twenty Middle Easterners, residing and being trained in Cuba, for an operation being planned against the U.S. very soon. The Cuban official that we were listening to told his superior that the Chinese asked if the Arabs as they called them were already fluent in Spanish. He reported that they spoke Spanish as if they were Mexicans and had immersed themselves in the Mexican culture as well. The Cubans called it Operation Black Swan. I have no details of it; however, the Cubans are to bring these men on their cargo ship and transfer them to the Da Dan Xian. Then, when the ship makes port at Lazaro Cardenas in Mexico, these guys will disembark and make their way to Brownsville and other cities in Texas, with the help of a Cuban shipping company that will pick them up—covertly, of course."

"Wow, this guy said all that on the phone?" asked Alex.

"Well, they were on a sat phone, but the guy here was very nervous as he related all the information to his superior. I think he wanted to get it all out before he forgot it, or something," she replied, acknowledging the fresh cup of coffee that Joey had made for her with a smile and a thumbs-up.

"This is very timely and important information. I will relay it immediately and I am sure the CIA and the Department of Homeland Security will be all over it. You guys did a great job. I need John and Joey back here ASAP. However, Jackie and Mel ... Is everybody there?" Alex asked. They all responded to the affirmative in unison. "Great, you even sound like a chorus now. Anyway, Jackie and Mel, I need you to stay behind for a few days. My fiancée, Miss Julia—by the way you missed the engagement—is going to be in Mexico City for a couple of days on business. I would like you guys to accompany her and return together."

"Viva Mexico! Party time! Congratulations to both of you! Tell you what," said Jackie as she looked at Mel. "We now know some caliente places where we can have a bachelorette party for Miss Julia."

"Maybe I should leave John and Joey behind instead," said Alex, laughing.

"We got this, Boss," said Mel.

"Very well, guys, good work. John and Joey, I'll see you guys bright and early tomorrow. Thank you all. Over and out," he said, as he hung up.

"I think you should call your boyfriend, Arturo, and pay him a visit to thank him for all the information he gave us," said Mel.

"No, not after what little I saw of him on that video. Thank you. Mel and I are going to hit the town tonight, while you muchachos have to fly back to the Windy City and work. See ya," said Jackie, giving Mel a high ten with a broad smile.

"Tell me about this FARC group," said Melissa, as she followed Jackie to their room with Joey trailing behind.

"In my prior life as a DEA agent, I had direct dealings with the FARC," said Jackie, as she moved back into her room and sat down. Both Mel and Joey were listening intently. "They were encouraged by the success of the Castro Communist revolution in Cuba. I think FARC was established in the early to mid 1960s, as part of the Colombia Communist Party. So, as you can see, they have been around for about forty years now. They have devastated numerous towns and villages in the rural and mountainous regions of Colombia where they operate. Tens of thousands have died as a result of their insurgency; many of the victims were innocent villagers, killed as a result of landmines buried around their encampments, and many more as a result of the civil war FARC has fomented for so many years," she went on.

"How do they finance such a long insurgency?" asked Joey.

"That's how my direct contact came in while at the DEA. The FARC has forced farmers for years to plant coca in their fields. That has been their main business. Second to the cocaine business is kidnapping for ransom. Gangs in the major cities in Mexico and other countries kidnap high net worth individuals and business people, regardless of their nationality, and then receive a finder's fee as they turn them over to FARC operatives. A little known fact is that many U.S. business people who travel abroad are provided by their employers with kidnap insurance through Lloyds of London, which makes them prime targets for these gangs. Once kidnapped, the employee calls an international number and their ransom is negotiated immediately. Usually, a flat $1 million," she said.

"Wow. That sounds like a fast-food service for kidnappers," quipped Mel.

"Absolutely," chimed in Joey.

"Sounds simple, but not all kidnappings go well and many have died while being held. However, it is big business," said Jackie, as she prepared to take a shower. "Joey, back to your room. I am going to take a shower, and you, my boy, have to pack."

CHAPTER TEN

Cartagena, Colombia

Listening to Jackie talk about Colombia and the drug business, I unfortunately had a flashback to an event in my life in 1994 that I would rather erase from my memory. Or, as Joey would say, hit the delete button.

On the outskirts of Cartagena and throughout many of the farmlands in Colombia, the farmers had been forced to plant coca. Most of the corn, coffee, and other crops had been converted into a very lucrative business for the drug cartels.

Emilio Nuñez, or Emilito as his mother called him, was the man of the house. At fourteen years old he had inherited a tremendous burden with deep sorrow in his heart. He was now responsible for his ill mother and eight-year-old brother, Manuelito.

Don Emilio, his father, had been a farmer. They owned a few acres and had farmed coffee for many years, going back to when Don Emilio's father, now deceased, had worked the farm and was able to buy a few acres for himself and the family. The family was not rich, but they made an honest living and were able to enjoy the necessities of life without any fanfare or extravagance. After all, this little village had very few amenities to offer.

Because of his religious convictions and animosity

towards drugs, Don Emilio resisted the cartels' mandates to convert his meager coffee fields to coca. For the cartels it was not a matter of choice, and allowing Don Emilio to refuse would send a message of weakness to the other farmers. Instead, the cartels sent a chilling message when they gunned down Don Emilio outside the village chapel after services on a Sunday morning.

Emilito was promised that his family could keep the land and be paid a guaranteed monthly sum as long as coca was planted in the fields and he helped the cartels with anything they demanded. They even offered him a large lump sum, payable to his mother, should something happen to him while in their employ as long as the land became the property of the cartels.

Hands trembling, sitting motionless in the red mud, I rested my back against the boulder I had used for cover and leverage. My vision was blurred, out of focus. The only things I could see clearly were the drops of rainwater as they slid down the brim of my Dallas Cowboys' 1994 championship Super Bowl cap. My head hung low in repentance. Drop by drop, the rain slowly dripped on my M24 Remington sniper rifle that lay across my lap. What the fuck had I done? The last time I had cried was when my mother passed away three years earlier. Broken-hearted at my inability to attend her funeral, I shed the tears and wondered when was the last time I had told her I loved her.

My face was covered with raindrops so I pretended the tears were also raindrops. But there was no denying the tears; they had a distinct salty taste that my mouth revealed instantly upon receiving them.

Lightning illuminated the sky, but I wasn't looking. Thunder crashed seconds later; I could hear it, but I wasn't listening. The storm had moved in suddenly over the valley below me. It was as if my actions had awakened the Almighty and I had made Him mad. Somehow He was telling me how He felt about the completion of my mission. Now, after a successful kill, I felt empty, isolated, and remorseful... a considerable contrast to my feelings after other kills when I experienced exhilaration and a rush of adrenaline after pulling the trigger.

Tilting my head back against the boulder, I could see the dissonance of colors in the still mad sky. Blue and black it was, with streaks of gray, orange, yellow, and red in what my artsy friends would call a modern abstract painting, void of figurative reality.

The wind calmed down, and I could see the raindrops as they fell on my face and dawdled on my thick and dirty blond beard.

A second explosion in the small village below startled me. I couldn't look. My hands reached up to my face to wipe the raindrops away, and yes, the tears. It was time for me to get the fuck out and reach my extraction point. But what had I done? Had I caused the first explosion? Had I killed them all? I retrieved my gear and my M24 and without looking down, I walked away.

My Delta Force team was in Cartagena, Colombia. We had information about a drug cartel boss and we were on the chase. A local, risking his life, had informed the Colombian military that the cartel had set a trap for us in this village just outside of Cartagena. Different from the SEALs, whose missions are normally documented—the key word here is normally—Delta tends to work covertly for the most part. Our work in Colombia, while known to many, was not an official function of the U.S. government. We were happy to do it and the Colombian government was happy to let us do it. Because of that, the Colombian military was nowhere near where we were operating today. My job was to be on overwatch, as our team consisting of twelve Delta Force specialists, including myself, made our way in three Humvees through the village. One of my specialties with the team was being a sniper. I had traveled ahead and positioned myself on a hill with a perfect vantage point of the village in the valley below. Once our team crossed the village, I would join them at a preplanned extraction point, and we would continue our trek towards Cartagena.

Normally, I do my job and move on. I don't look back or give it much thought after completion. As a sniper, I can't continuously replay my kills. It's bad enough that my targets visit me once in a while when I sleep. Because of what occurred in this village, I found the need to revisit the event and find out who this boy was and why he did what he did. A year later, I was able to find out more about who had been my target that day.

The cartels recruited young boys for their use by any means possible. To the cartels, they were merely pawns and in some cases simply tools to carry out their terror in the local streets and in cities. Expendable was a more accurate description of what these young boys really were to these criminals.

That evening Emilito had been assigned to carry explosives—a bomb—to be placed as an IED or improvised explosive device on the road by an abandoned car. The targets were my guys riding in three U.S. Special Forces Humvees.

I had been on overwatch at the top of the small mountain surrounding the valley that was the home to this little village...just a few miles from the city of Cartagena. As I looked down from my vantage point about eight hundred or so yards away, I was reminded of a training exercise in New Mexico. The town looked like an Old West town from the 1880's, a few buildings made of red clay and wood, the main street with its stores, a chapel, and local businesses aligned on each side and a small red dirt road that was the central point for the town. This was an easy shot for me, a trained Delta Force specialist.

At about seven p.m., just as the sun was setting and mere seconds before the storm overtook the valley, I spotted two young boys and an older boy coming out of a home near an abandoned car. To my amazement, the older boy was strapping a vest with explosives on the boy I came to know was Emilito. A typical Colombian cape in vivid colors was then draped around his shoulders concealing the explosives. The older boy placed both boys on the street with a ball and motioned for them to kick it back and forth. I could see through my binoculars that both young boys wore Yankees' baseball caps on their heads.

I had only one option. Placing my Remington M24 on the boulder, I took aim as I looked at Emilito's face through my scope and saw a face full of terror as he awaited the inevitable. Momentarily closing my eyes and asking for forgiveness, I slowly pulled back the trigger of my M24 sniper rifle. It was a few seconds before Emilito's head exploded from my single bullet as thunder roared in the valley. The second young boy's scream could be heard echoing in the town as other men, women, and children began running out of their homes and encircled the remains of Emilito within seconds of the shot. As the convoy with my guys was turning the corner, Emilito's body exploded, killing instantly all the bystanders—yes, all the men, women, and children. The older boy, excited and nervous, was hiding in a nearby bodega and detonated the explosives remotely.

I could not believe my eyes. Mayhem, death, and destruction were displayed in front of me as a result of my one shot. Sitting in the red mud and resting my wet, shivering, and beaten body against the boulder, I turned my soaked cap to face the front. I could only focus on the raindrops as they fell from my brim in front of me onto my Remington M24 sniper rifle resting on my lap.

"John, are you OK?" asked Joey, walking back into our room.

"Yeah. Why do you ask?" I replied.

"You look like you are going to pass out, man. You are as white as the bed sheets."

"I'm OK, kid. Still recovering from yesterday, I guess." These memories, like some others I wished to forget, would occasionally come back to haunt me. Jackie had triggered this one by speaking about drugs and Colombia. "Let's pack and get out of here, kid," I said, walking into the bathroom to take a cold shower.

CHAPTER ELEVEN

Chicago, Illinois

"So, I heard you lined up sitters for me while I'm in Mexico City," said Julia as Alex hung up the phone.

"Indeed. Jackie and Melissa will stay behind and meet you at the airport when you arrive. Do you mind?" Alex asked.

"No, not at all. They are very nice and professional. It will be nice to have company while I'm there those two days," she said as she finished packing her suitcase. "I've spoken to my hosts in Mexico and told them I have a ride from the airport. They were going to pick me up and take me to the hotel."

"This is simple; you are staying at the Presidente Hotel. That's exactly where Jackie and Mel are staying. I'll just have them extend their stay for a couple of days," he said. "And by the way, do not wear any expensive jewelry while in Mexico."

"Got that. Not to change the subject, but the other part of the conversation sounded very serious," she said, rubbing his shoulders as he sat behind his desk in his studio and waited for a callback from the CIA.

"Enough so that I think that Homeland Security will raise the threat level," Alex said.

"That serious?" she inquired, moving around to the

front of his desk to see his face.

"Yes, that serious. The report is that there are Islamic terrorists who have been training in Cuba and are about to infiltrate the southern Texas border via Mexico posing as Mexicans," he said. "We have been expecting a second wave of attacks after the Twin Towers—perhaps this is it."

"Well, if the CIA and Homeland play their cards right, they should be able to intercept them before or as they cross the border, don't you think?" she asked, looking into his eyes with a look of concern.

"The information we've got is crucial to that success. Can you imagine if..." Alex was saying as his phone rang. "This is the CIA in conference with Homeland. Let me get this."

Julia went about her business, finishing her packing. She had a flight out of Chicago's O'Hare Airport in a few hours, taking her direct to Benito Juarez International Airport in Mexico City. She listened as Alex relayed the information, first about the potential infiltration of the Middle Easterners and then about the military cargo being diverted to Venezuela for the FARC, also known as the Marxist rebel group, the Revolutionary Armed Forces of Colombia. Julia went on with her packing, making sure to select her "fantasy" jewelry to wear in Mexico. She had done this before. Any expensive jewelry, a Rolex, or other well-known expensive watch could immediately target her for a mugging, or even worse, a kidnapping. She waited for Alex to conclude his conversation as she e-mailed some of her friends and associates about her trip to Mexico City, the dates she would be out, and her return date and time.

"Well, that was an intense conversation," said Alex as he hung up the phone.

"Who with?" asked Julia, as she looked around to make sure she had not forgotten anything.

"George Tenet and Tom Ridge."

"You are talking to the top guys these days. From an NOC at the CIA to reporting to the top of the food chain," she said, laughing. "You've come a long way for a *Cubanito de Miami,* Alejandro," she said, rubbing his hair and messing it up.

"I guess I have. Tenet is DCI, or Director of Intelligence for the CIA, and Ridge is Assistant to the President for Homeland Security. Anyway, they are very interested in the possible incursion of the Middle Easterners into Texas. They are going to try to set something up to prevent that from happening," he said.

"Next thing you know, you'll be on the phone with W.," she said, as she continued to tease Alex. "What about the shipment for FARC?"

"They'll pass that along to the Colombian authorities. Nothing they want to get involved in at this time."

"So, are you going to miss me?" she asked, tilting her

head to the right as her full head of long blonde hair moved in unison with her body.

Looking at her made him sigh. “Yes, I will miss you, especially after that celebration last night. I guess I should have proposed long ago.”

“Well, go to Victoria’s Secret and get me a surprise or two—for when I come back,” she said, with a suggestive look on her face.

“Right after I drop you off at O’Hare. You bet.”

“Well, so you know, I am going to miss you, too—a lot. I love you,” she said, looking into his eyes and smiling tenderly.

“And I love you,” he said softly.

CHAPTER TWELVE

Havana, Cuba

Colonel Abimbola was conducting a raid along the Paseo del Malecón, a main thoroughfare in downtown Havana that bordered the Atlantic Ocean and served as a backdrop for the historic hotels that lined this once beautiful boulevard. Foamy white waves were crashing over the seawall with fury and vengeance as if to protest the atrocities being conducted in their presence. The bright blue sky above them was also a witness to the aggression. Freedom-loving Cubans had gathered in the heat of the day to protest the incarceration of one of their leaders. They carried homemade signs and repeated in unison the same words, *"No mas arrestos"* or "no more arrests." Others stood by emotionless... frozen in fear for their own lives if they dared to say anything or look with empathy at the beatings being administered by the police.

Colonel Abimbola stood and smiled. With his six-foot-four-inch frame, he was an imposing figure in his olive green uniform and the beret he preferred to a hat. He was silent, but his commands were understood. "Beat the sons of bitches to submission, create fear, and chill the rest of the bystanders."

These demonstrations were becoming more and more common and Abimbola was determined to quash them every time. The dissidents were powerless. No organized rebellions, no guns, bombs, or any acts of violence against the oppressive Communist regime were within their grasp. The regime, in turn, had led an organized rebellion in the late 1950s, just prior to coming into power. Daily bombings at movie theaters, restaurants, assassinations, and every act of terror imaginable, were committed indiscriminately on the citizenry. These acts of terror had worked for them back in the '50s. They learned their lesson well.

Abimbola's phone rang as he stood and continued to watch with disdain as the thrashings were administered. "This is Abimbola," he said loudly into the phone.

"Colonel, this is Captain Ruiz. We have news on the whereabouts of Julia Muller and Jackie Allison," he said.

"Captain, let me get in my vehicle; I cannot hear you very well," he said, as he climbed into his Russian made UAZ-469 jeep, nicknamed *Kozlik*, or Goat. "Go ahead, Captain."

"Colonel, we intercepted e-mails from Julia Muller. She is on her way to Mexico City. She will be there for two days, and best yet, Jackie Allison will be with her. Plus a third person we have not identified," said the captain.

"Excellent work, Captain. Could the third person be Alejandro Cardenas?" he asked, hoping it was.

"No, sir. From the e-mails, we know that Cardenas will remain in Chicago," the captain replied.

"Well, once we have Julia, he'll come to us like a little dog in heat, looking for his mate," said Abimbola, laughing. "Captain, meet me at headquarters. We'll plan the kidnapping and extraction of Julia and Jackie from there. In the meantime, contact the Jimenez cartel in Mexico City. Tell them to stand by, that we have a job for them in the city tomorrow. Go ahead and give the cartel the information you already have on Julia and Jackie's whereabouts. I'll contact them later with the final plan for extraction from Mexico to good old Cuba. You know, Captain, I've been thinking about this agent, Jackie, since you showed me her picture," he said, as he grabbed his manhood. "Mano, I can't wait to have her in my custody; she's become an obsession of mine. "*¡Que rica esta!*"

He told his driver to leave the scene of the beatings and return to headquarters. The police knew what to do with the dissidents. He personally didn't give a shit.

The Colonel had waited two years for this revenge. "Revenge is a dish best served cold," he said to himself, quoting from the novel, Les Liaisons Dangereuses, written by Pierre Choderlos de Laclos in 1782, in which the novelist wrote, *"La vengeance eat un plat qui se mange froid."* Abimbola removed his red-beret, closed his eyes, and rested his head against the headrest.

CHAPTER THIRTEEN

Chicago, Illinois

I knew that Alex arrived early in his office. Many times he had asked me to be there at five-thirty in the morning. I was used to it while serving with Delta and the CIA, but maybe I was getting lazy in my old age. Alex loved seeing the sunrise overlooking Lake Michigan as the sunrays slowly crept up the floor and walls of his office until the entire office was illuminated with a red-and-orange glow. He would stand and gaze through the wall-to-wall glass panes, as the lake itself became an artist's canvass, with the vivid colors being slowly stroked by a painter with an incredible imagination. Some mornings he would call up to Julia's office to see if she was enjoying the sunrise. Today, however, he would have to merely tell her when she called from Mexico. These two had a love for each other that I longed for. Maybe soon, I could find my soul mate. Or, maybe just a mate.

After Joey and I walked in, Alex gave us his agenda for our meeting. The first order of business involved meeting with Joey to begin the investigation of the N.A. Ltd. Hedge Fund. Alex had planned on traveling to New York later in the day to sit down personally with Nikolas Akakios, assuming that he could get an appointment with him. His plan was to confront Akakios and test the waters by telling him that his competitors had suspicions that perhaps someone in Akakios's organization was conducting corporate espionage against them. It was not so much that he wanted to give him the benefit of the doubt. He actually wanted to see his reaction.

His intercom beeped.

"Mr. C., I have Mr. David Casselback on the phone for you, sir," Joy, his assistant, said.

"Thank you, Joy. Put him on," he replied as he moved behind his desk and sat down to take the incoming call.

"Guys, have a seat on the sofa. I'll be with you in a few minutes," he told us.

"Alex, this is Special Agent in Charge David Casselback with the FBI. Good morning to you," Casselback said.

"Special Agent, good morning. Pleasure speaking with you, sir. I have two of my operatives that uncovered the information yesterday in Mexico with me now in the office. Do you mind if I put you on speaker phone?"

"No, not at all. Go ahead and do so. Please call me David. I have heard a lot about you, and have been looking forward to one day meeting you. Unfortunately, I did not want it to be under these circumstances. Also, guys, great work!" Casselback said.

"Thank you, that's very kind of you. What can I help you with?"

"Let me get to the point. As you know, time is of the

essence with respect to the information you uncovered yesterday. You know what I mean?" Casselback asked.

"Yes, I do."

"Fine. Can you spare John Powers for a few days?" Casselback inquired.

Joey looked at me and smiled. He whispered, "You're the big dog."

Alex thought for a second and said, "Why, yes, I can. How long will you need him?"

"I don't know exactly. We are shorthanded, as you can imagine, and I need every available experienced person that can be of help to us on the field right now," replied Casselback.

"Where do you need him, and when?" asked Alex looking at me now.

"Today. ASAP. In Brownsville, Texas. He should report to the FBI field office there. I will be there to greet him," Casselback said.

"Can you use additional experienced personnel? I have three more guys with the same qualifications as John that I could provide," Alex added.

"You bet, Alex. That's splendid. In that case, have the team drive to our office in Chicago. We'll fly them there. I really appreciate that," Casselback said. "We'll discuss payment later, of course."

"Not a problem, David; I'm on retainer with DOD and

happy to be of service. John is here now, and I'll alert the others."

"Thank you," said Casselback as Alex hung up the phone.

I saw Alex sit back in his chair and look at the ceiling in his office as he pondered all that was happening. The threat that these extremist jihadists could enter the U.S. to carry out whatever plan they had been trained for was serious. Every agency was on alert for what was expected— a second wave of terror. The days after the 9/11 attacks were somber moments; the attack had exemplified how vulnerable our country was to terrorists. They only had to be right one time, as they had shown on that unforgettable day. Yet it was incumbent on our defense systems to be right 100 percent of the time, an insurmountable task of extreme proportions. Alex told Joy to alert the three-team members that would be accompanying me on this mission.

"I am glad you guys are here," Alex said, as he sat up in his chair. "Joey, give me a minute to deal with a major development that John needs to attend to, but stay there on the sofa. I need you for an assignment.

"John, after you gather your things, pick up Javier, Dan, and Tom and go to the FBI office on Roosevelt Road."

"Two ex-Deltas and two ex-SEALs. This is serious, Boss," I replied.

"It is, John. I don't know how long you'll be gone. From

what we heard, you and the others are being embedded with the FBI counterterrorist unit to assist in the search and capture of the men attempting to enter the U.S. through Texas. The same men that you guys uncovered were being smuggled into Mexico from the Chinese freighter, the Da Dan Xia," said Alex looking straight at John.

"What about gear?" I asked.

"Take your personal stuff only. Casselback will take care of the rest, I am sure," Alex replied. "I'll have someone drive all four of you. Keep me posted if you can."

"I'm getting a flashback to old times, Boss," I said. "I'm out of here. Later, Joey."

"Be safe, Hulk," said Joey as I walked out of Alex's office. "And, Major, go for it."

"Thanks, kid," I replied as I walked out of the room on my way to Texas.

Alex got up from his desk and walked around to sit with Joey in a more comfortable chair by the sofa. "Are you ready for a task requiring your abilities with the computer and cyberspace?" asked Alex.

"Always," replied Joey with a smile.

"Good. We are investigating the possibility of corporate espionage and potential hacking by a company in New York called N.A. Limited, owned by Nikolas Akakios."

"The Nikolas Akakios?" Joey asked.

"I don't know of more than one, do you?"

"Sorry, I was just surprised. Please go ahead," Joey said.

Alex went on to explain the concerns they had about Akakios in every detail. "I am going to meet with Mr. Akakios, perhaps today or in a couple of days, and I need to be fully informed," Alex said.

"How deep do you want to me to ... let me say, investigate," asked Joey cautiously.

"Like I said, I need to be fully informed. Specifically, I need to see his stock trading activity, with attention to the trades that are made against the markets or individual stocks. Those are called short sales. Do I need to elaborate?"

"No, I understand," replied Joey.

Alex got up from his chair, signaling the briefing was over. Smiling and extending a handshake to Joey, he said, "Welcome back, kid. Go do your thing and report back as soon as possible. This is an urgent matter."

"On my way, sir. Mexico was fun, but it is always good to come back to the States," said Joey as he walked out of Alex's office.

Alex went back to sit behind his desk. He reached for the phone and dialed Julia's number. He waited patiently as her voice mail answered, asking him to leave a message. He dialed Jackie's phone, similarly to no avail. Voice mail again. He left her a message.

He was a little surprised that neither had answered. He

called Joy on the intercom. “Joy, see if you can reach Melissa. I’ve tried Julia and Jackie, but I’m only getting their voice mails. Let me know if you get her. “Thanks,” he said with a little bit of trepidation in his voice. He leaned back in his chair as an icy feeling overtook him.

CHAPTER FOURTEEN

New York City

Nikolas Akakios sat in his dark office with the head trader of his very successful N.A. Ltd. Hedge Fund. Hedge funds were considered alternative investments and the managers of these funds had flexibility in deciding how to allocate the investments. A fund would be created with pooled money from investors, whether individual or institutional, with the specific goal of creating a better return than that of the general market. The manager of the hedge fund usually charged a fee plus a percentage of the profits generated. Most of these trades were very large and done in what was referred to as "dark pools" with little or no transparency to the individual investors. Akakios had set up one of the very few dark pools in existence in 2002.

"Stewart, we are going to begin a series of short sales today to be closed at the end of the day, regardless of the outcome on various stocks and indices," said Akakios, as he looked down at his file reviewing his information. "Please make a note of the following: Sell one million shares short of the following three banks, Allen Bank, Country Bank, and SunMarc Bank. Got it?"

"Yes, sir," replied Stewart. "Will there be anything else?"

"Sell one million shares short of the following: Elo

Teck, World Micro, and Placid Electronics. There's more," he added. "Sell one million shares short of Super Stores, CostMart, and Allmart."

"Understood. We are selling one million shares short of nine securities at the market for the duration of today, to be closed and bought back at the end of the day," Stewart repeated.

"Very good. Now, tomorrow morning reverse these trades on the nine stocks and buy them long for one day only. Also, Stewart, I want you to go long and buy options on the Nikkei and the Dax indices, one million each to hold until further notice."

"I'll execute these immediately, sir," Stewart said.

"How is the family?" asked Akakios, closing his file and looking up at his trader with a smile.

"Very well, sir. Thank you for asking," replied Stewart.

"Excellent. Go on your way then. Let me know when we are done."

"Yes, Mr. Akakios."

Akakios had grown fond of Stewart. He found him to be quiet, reserved, and most importantly, faithful to him. After Stewart's five years in his employ, Akakios had never had an occasion to doubt his dedication.

Marta Oliva, Akakios's confidante, walked into his office and closed the door. "You wanted to discuss something?" she asked.

"Yes, have a seat," he replied. Picking up a pink message note on his desk, he continued, "Have you ever heard of Alejandro "Alex" Cardenas. I understand he is Cuban."

"No, I've never heard of him. Cardenas is a somewhat common last name. Why do you ask?"

"Well, he has asked for an appointment to see me. In checking, I see he runs a security and intelligence business called Sect-Intel. I have no idea why he would want to talk to me. But I am a bit curious."

"More than likely he wants to offer his services personally to you."

"Perhaps. But I have a feeling it is more than that. I'll have my assistant set it up. When he shows up, I want you in the room with me. You have good eyes, my dear, and I'll need your counsel on this one."

"I'll consult my saints prior to his arrival. Do you have a picture of him?"

"Go onto his website and print one up. Then do what you do," he said, as he smiled at her. "We are getting closer to achieving my dream and that of our group's, Marta."

"Do you think Operation Black Swan will achieve that?"

"It's the beginning. When chaos reigns in the world economies, when the people of the world get to the point of despair, then they will clamor for us to restore order and provide for them. We will have one world order by controlling the riches of the world and providing structure for all. Plus, we will serve the essential needs for every citizen of the world: a decent living, health care, schooling for children, a job, and the best freedom of all—freedom from fear," said Akakios in a preacher-like mode.

"Can you trust the Chinese?" asked Marta.

"The Chinese government has the most experience in controlling the masses. They have moved into a pseudo-capitalist system, allowing the growth of the middle class while still having central control. That is the key. The partnership that will be created between us, the elite thinkers around the world and this one world government, will be like no other ever seen. They need us to manage the world economies and we need them to manage the citizenry. We take care of them, they take care of us, and together, we take care of the world. Trust is not an issue. We respect each other, and we know what each partner brings to the table. There is a Chinese proverb that says, 'vicious as a tigress can be, she never eats her own cubs.' That is the mantra we need to apply."

"I hope the Chinese are like the tigress, and not the scorpion and you the frog. That is my fear," Marta replied.

CHAPTER FIFTEEN

Mexico City

Julia arrived in the late afternoon at Benito Juarez International Airport in Mexico City where Jackie and Melissa were waiting for her. After collecting her luggage and clearing customs, they headed to the elevator through the airport lobby, full of stores and money exchange booths. The elevator would take them to the aboveground parking lot to retrieve their car. Jackie's training kept her vigilant for anything unexpected that might be around them. Melissa, although new to the tradecraft, had quickly learned from Jackie and stayed back a few feet from both Julia and Jackie.

Entering the large elevator, they soon realized they were crammed inside with twelve other people as they rode to the fourth floor of the parking garage. Jackie felt very uncomfortable in such a small compartment and looked with suspicious eyes at every occupant. There was no imminent threat, but her training was such that she felt uneasy about the ride.

Julia was at ease, however. Her carefree nature and the happiness she was feeling about her engagement made her vulnerable to any unforeseen danger that might be lurking. "Are we headed to the Hotel Presidente now?" she asked, as everyone in the otherwise quiet elevator looked at her.

Melissa was about to respond in the affirmative, as Jackie said, “No, we’ve grown tired of the Presidente We have a surprise in store for you. After all, we have a bachelorette party to attend.”

Julia in her naïve way replied, “Oh. But, Alex said ...”

Not wanting Julia to continue, Jackie broke in, “Alex, your husband-to-be, wants you at a business hotel. ... boring. We have another type of business in mind. Fiesta time!” Jackie said loudly as almost everyone smiled in the elevator except for two short poorly dressed men who had gotten in the elevator last.

The three ladies exited the elevator on their way to the car. Both Jackie and Melissa were aware that the two men also exited the elevator on their floor. Melissa dropped back a few steps and slid her hand into an over-the-shoulder bag she carried and clutched a Glock 19. Because of its reduced size, the weapon was an excellent choice for concealing in her bag and she had become very proficient in its use. Jackie led the way to their car, as the two men seemed lost in the parking structure. Melissa kept a vigilant eye on them.

“Julia, please get in the backseat,” Jackie said, as she opened the door for Julia before opening the driver’s side door and getting in. She started the car, pulled out of the parking space, and drove about ten yards towards the exit as Melissa opened the passenger door and got in the slow-moving vehicle. Losing sight of the men, they began to drive out, but prior to stopping at the booth to pay, Mel stepped out of the car again and walked alongside with her hand in her bag. Just as Jackie paid, Mel got back in the car. Jackie made a left turn into traffic, and they were on their way to Mexico City.

"You guys are scaring me," said Julia from the backseat. "You could be working for the Secret Service the way you carry yourselves."

"The rule is simple: Prepare for the worst and hope for the best," Jackie replied, as she made her way through the crazy traffic.

"Are we not going to the Presidente Hotel?" Julia asked.

"I think we are. I just didn't want to give anyone a clue unnecessarily," replied Jackie, looking back through her rearview mirror. "Mel, did you get a look at their car?'

"Did not. I lost them after I got in," Mel responded, as she looked back from the passenger's side rearview mirror. "It was probably nothing."

"So, what are the plans, ladies?" Julia asked.

"Your e-mail said that your appointment is tomorrow at noon. Is that correct?" asked Jackie.

"Yes, it is," replied Julia.

"Very well. In that case, I would rather get out of the city tonight. I've made reservations at a beautiful place in

Cuernavaca called Las Mañanitas. It's about an hour-and-a-half drive from the city," said Jackie, as she made a series of turns and exits in and out of the expressway while continuing to check on her rear.

"I've heard of that place. What a great idea! Do you want to drive that far?" Julia asked.

"We have a driver all set up. He'll drive us over and pick us up after breakfast tomorrow in time to drive back and be at your appointment on time," Jackie said. "This place has only twenty-nine rooms, all suites, very quaint. It's a hacienda built in 1955 in Mexican colonial style. The gardens are magnificent, with wild peacocks roaming around and aromatic flowers of all colors surrounding the stonewall perimeter. I was there a number of times during my work here in Mexico."

"Sounds like you have some good memories of the place," chimed in Melissa.

"Well, it was work. But it is a very romantic place if you want it to be. Know what I mean, girl?" Jackie added.

"Why is it that I can't connect to the States? I keep getting this annoying lady about metro cell ... or something," said Julia, as she tried calling on her cell.

"When in Mexico, Miss Julia," Jackie began. "You need to set up your phone for international calls in the States. Did you that?"

"I am sure I did at some point."

"Our phones don't work everywhere, either. Are you dialing 01 before calling the States?" inquired Jackie.

"I'll call from the hotel before we leave for Cuernavaca," Julia replied.

At the Presidente Hotel, Jackie and Melissa got their rooms and began packing their belongings while Julia freshened up.

"Jackie, on second thought, I think driving one-and-one-half hours to Cuernavaca makes no sense tonight. We would then have to drive back tomorrow for my meeting," began Julia. "Let's stay here tonight. I'll go to my meeting tomorrow, and then we'll take a ride out and stay at Las Mañanitas one night. We can enjoy the afternoon and evening there. How's that?"

"Works for me, Miss Julia. I'll call and change our reservations to tomorrow. We'll have an early dinner tonight. Any preference?" asked Jackie.

"Well, you know, Alex is not big on steak or beef, for that matter. Any good steak houses?" Julia replied.

"Got just the place. Sir Winston Churchill's. Not too far from us. It's an old English mansion turned into a steak house in the middle of the city. If you like prime rib, this is the place," said Jackie.

"From the name, I am sure they have good scotch also. I am in. Mel, is that good with you?" asked Julia.

"Am in, ladies. Steak and spirits," replied Mel.

"Great. I'll go to the lobby and check in. Wait for you ladies there," said Julia.

CHAPTER SIXTEEN

Brownsville, Texas

The afternoon sunrays, orange and yellow in a bright and vibrant form, came in at an angle of about forty-five degrees through every oval window on the right side of the airplane. We could see each projection of light creating a unique picture on the opposite side of the cabin. The sunrays momentarily mesmerized me as the angle of projection changed to match the angle of descent of the plane. We arrived in Brownsville, Texas—Javier, Dan, Tom and I—aboard the Gulfstream the FBI had provided for us. A black Chevy Suburban was waiting for us at the small private airport known as Resaca Airstrip, four miles from downtown. I was getting used to the comforts of the Gulfstream. I had fallen in love with the agent acting as a flight attendant. I was very glad the agent was a female with her large emerald green eyes and her jet-black hair ... Wow! The free drinks had a lot to do with my feelings, but it was time to go to work. Stepping out of the plane, I could feel the heat and dryness on my face. Sweat instantly overtook me along with an immediate momentary flashback to the Middle East. Our driver, Agent Ray Thompson, welcomed us aboard and, as he drove, told us that we were headed to a Holiday Inn where the FBI had set up a temporary field office and had arranged accommodations for us. I was hoping that we each had a room; I liked my privacy and, having been with Javier, my fellow Delta brother, on other missions, I knew he snored up a storm. Dan and Tom, well, they like to stick together, being SEALs and all. What do they say? Birds of a feather, etc.

Agent Ray brought us up to speed on the way.

"Guys, we've been here a day already," Agent Ray began. "We have not had much luck. We believe these men are going to be using the same tunnels used by the drug cartels to smuggle themselves into the U.S."

"Ray, are you stationed here in Brownsville?" I asked.

"Yes, I am. We have a small field office that we have outgrown since 9/11," he replied.

"So, I gather you know some of the bad hombres in town?"

"We've rounded up the usual suspects related to drug smuggling and have been questioning them for a day," he responded.

"And anything from that?" I inquired and followed up with, "Have you been asking or interrogating?"

"Asking. We really have no real suspects to interrogate at this point," Agent Ray replied.

"So, what's the plan?"

"Special Agent in Charge David Casselback is waiting for us at the Holiday Inn. He will brief everyone as to the nature of the ops."

"Do we have to call him Special Agent in Charge David Casselback?" I asked, hoping this guy was not a hard-ass. I had always wondered why some agents were special, and others were not. I mean, if "special" meant a better agent, why not make all the agents special? Right? Just saying.

"Nothing to worry about there. He is cool," he said. "Any of you guys speak Spanish?"

"I speak a little. Javi back there, better known as '*La Puta*,' is a native of Merida, Mexico. Dan and Tom, they just don't speak at all. They are SEALs," I said, turning around and looking at the guys with a big smile that they did not return in kind. "They clap a lot." Dan gave me the finger as I said that.

"Good. I am sure the director will keep you together since you can communicate if we cross the border," Agent Ray said.

"FBI crossing the border?" I asked.

"Well, we have FBI, DEA, ICE, and a couple more agencies and groups working together. But you guys are independents; you can pretty much do anything and go anywhere. Comprende, amigos?" Agent Ray replied.

"Are we going to be told that officially?" I asked.

"I was asked to mention that to you. And, no, you are not going to be told that officially," he replied.

"*Mucho comprende*," I said, again looking back at the guys as all three nodded their understanding.

We arrived at the Holiday Inn in the middle of nowhere and close to nothing. Had the town moved away or were the owners of the Holiday Inn planning for growth? Build it and they will come? I didn't think so. A new expressway had moved the traffic away from this motel. I guess they didn't have the best lobbyist when they built it. So the Holiday Inn was delighted to have become, albeit temporarily, the FBI Brownsville's field office for counterterrorism. Agent Ray showed us to our rooms. Excellent. Four rooms, one for each of us, but no minibar. Well, we were officially on duty. Cervezas later, I hoped for. We had a briefing planned for 1600 hours—that's four in the afternoon—in the hotel's conference room that was now our operations center. Having a few minutes to kill, I decided to call Jackie who was in Mexico City with Julia and Mel. Got nothing but voice mail. I left no message. She was busy, and so I would be shortly.

A few minutes before 1600 hours my team walked into the conference room. Everyone stopped talking and turned around to look at us. Some of the looks I didn't care for. But I guess four strangers walking into a room full of agents of one kind or another would get some concerned looks.

"Gentlemen, welcome," said a handsome man of about fifty or so, who greeted us with a broad smile.

I assumed this was Special Agent in Charge David Casselback. At least, I was hoping it was. This guy looked friendly. He seemed jovial. Damn, he was good-looking, with deep intense green eyes, a full head of white hair neatly combed, and perfect teeth. He was slim and about six feet two inches tall. Shit, he looked "country clubbish." I would expect him to be the club president at Augusta National or something like that. I'd join his club just to hang out with him.

I extended my hand. "Pleasure to meet you, sir," I said. He returned the handshake with a strong grip and a smile with a full showing of his ultra white teeth.

"Major John Powers, I presume?" he asked.

"Yes, sir," I replied. I was still looking at the teeth.

"May I have your attention, please," said the special agent in charge, getting everyone's attention in the room. "This is retired Delta Force Major John Powers and his team who will be joining us on this operation. Major, please introduce the rest of your team."

And so I did. As I mentioned Delta Force and the SEALs, the faces around us began to change more to acceptance, except for one guy who quipped, "Mercenaries, Special Agent?"

The director laughed, looking at me and shaking his head. "Foreign Legionnaires," he replied, laughing. "Guys, gather around me," he said, motioning with both hands to the four of us, as if to signal that we should make a huddle around him. This guy must have been the quarterback of his

Ivy League college. Was I developing a man crush?

"Let me bring you up to date on the situation around here," he began. He gave us a full briefing on what they had done and what the plan was. It was imperative that these twenty jihadists be stopped before they crossed the border and scattered in the U.S.

"Special Agent Casselback," I began.

"Please call me David," he said.

Nice, we were on a first name basis. "David, can we talk to the few suspects you are holding?"

"Special Agent, that may not be prudent," said some stiff neck. This guy looked like he came from central casting for bureaucrats working on the fourth floor of the State Department. What a fuckhead. "We need to consider the legal ramifications of allowing these men, who are not government agents, to question the suspects," he went on.

All I am going to do is hang him by his testicles until they are torn away from his body. No, I didn't say that. Just wanted to. I suddenly realized that this asshole was the same one who had asked if we were mercenaries when we were first introduced. I wanted to pounce on this guy so bad. Casselback looked at me and with his eyes, pleaded for my patience.

"Mr. Ells, we are trying to gather information here to prevent a possible second major attack on our country. Major Powers and his men are not going to jeopardize the investigation," said Casselback, trying to remain calm himself. "Sure thing, John. We are holding them here with guards posted outside their doors." He motioned for us to follow him and ignored the asshole.

This Holiday Inn had everything. An operations center, dorm rooms, a prison, a mess hall with our own chef, and an armory from what I had been told.

So, me and Javi –*La Puta*, more on that later – walked into the room where we had been told a local gang leader was being detained. The man looked at us with disdain.

"What you want, *gringo de mierda*?" he said.

"*Pinche*, I'm no gringo," said Javi. "Stand up and take your shirt off."

The man followed orders. No reaction...just a very serious look. Javi went on to inspect his tattoos, looking at each one carefully.

"What's your name?" asked Javi.

Reluctantly, the man answered, "Roberto."

"Go ahead and put your shirt back on, Roberto. And sit down," Javi said, looking at me now.

"Roberto, let me tell you about yourself. You are a gang member and a member of a drug cartel. You have been in prison, both in the U.S. and in Mexico. So far, so good?

"Yeah, so what?" Roberto asked.

"Let me get to the point because we don't have much

time. We don't care about your gang or cartel affiliation. We are not here to deal with that. You know what happened in New York on 9/11, right?"

"Yeah," he replied.

"We know that the cartels are helping some men come across the border, Arab men disguised as mejicanos, to carry out another attack like the one in New York."

"I have nothing to do with that," said Roberto, raising his eyebrows.

"Maybe not. But you do know who and where."

"You don't stay alive around here by talking."

"Roberto ..." Javi started.

I had enough of this nice bullshit talk between these guys. "Fuck this shit. Are you guys going on a date or something? Get up, asshole," I said, pointing to Roberto.

Roberto looked at Javi for protection. He saw my eyes grow bigger with fury and disgust.

"What are you going to do, John? We are talking here," Javi said.

"Tie his fucking hands now," I said, looking at Roberto, with my eyes about to pop out. I could see the fear in Roberto's eyes. He kept looking at Javi in hopes he would help out. Javi went ahead and tied Roberto's hands behind his back with plastic zip ties.

I took Roberto's T-shirt and pulled it up so his face and head were covered.

"¿Que pasa? ¿Que haces?" Roberto asked frantically.

I walked him to the bathroom. "Get in the tub, hot shit," I said and held him while he stepped into the tub. "Sit." He sat, and I turned the water on. I pulled his legs forward and held his back, so he would not fall on his head. Now I had him facing up with his legs pointing against the wall of the tub and his back and head fully horizontal on the base of the tub. With his hands tied behind his back, his head was lower than his midsection. Perfect. I motioned to Javi to hold his legs against the wall.

"What are you doing?" Roberto screamed. "Fuck you and the FBI."

"Normally we have a doctor present so no one dies from this. But I had no time to call one now. I took the showerhead off. For a cheap motel, this showerhead was a handheld model with various settings for massage, mist, and who knows what else. I set it on strong and aimed it at Roberto's face. "One, two, three ..." I stopped. Roberto jumped and went into spasms, trying to kick with his legs and coughing and gasping for air.

"John, you are going to kill him," said Javi loudly, while smiling at me.

"What the fuck do I care. We have others who will tell us," I said into Roberto's wet covered face. He said nothing. I turned the water on again. Roberto's body stiffened as the water suffocated him again. "This time I am going to count until ten, not three like last time," I said, as I began to spray.

"A warehouse, a warehouse," Roberto shouted, as the spray reached his face.

I turned the water sideways but not off. "What warehouse?"

"Close to the border. There is a warehouse that stores food imports from Mexico."

"What is the name?" I asked, speaking slowly.

"Mexico Lindo Imports. There is a tunnel from Mexico," he said, breathing more regularly now. "I don't know anything else. Please stop."

"Javi, untie him. Let him get back to his room. I'll go see Casselback," I said, as I began walking out of the room.

These guys had questioned Roberto. How had they done it? Over beer and tacos? Walking into the director's office, I said, "Sir, we have a lead from one of the guys we talked to. We need to locate a warehouse for Mexico Lindo Imports. There is a tunnel on the premises where illegals and drugs, and, God help us, more have been coming in from Mexico."

Special Agent Casselback, somewhat surprised, looked up at me, "I won't ask how you got this intel. Get everyone ready. Let's move. Move! Move!"

"What did you do to this man?" asked Mr. Ells.

I replied, "Well, this gangbanger says he is now going

to be called el Chicano *chiclano*."

"What is that? She-clan-o?" asshole Ells asked.

"You need to ask someone who gives a shit and speaks Spanish, I guess," I replied, moving quickly behind the director.

The director was still looking at me as we hurried out of his office. "What? We just sat down comfortably and had some liquid refreshments. Nothing harmful. As a matter of fact, I think he mentioned he might want to join the FBI or something."

"What is a *chiclano*?" asked the special agent in charge out of earshot of Mr. Ells.

"A male person or animal with only one testicle," I replied, smiling.

Everyone was moving quickly in what seemed to be an organized but chaotic sequence of events. Someone shouted my name, and as I looked around, I saw they were pointing to a black Chevy Suburban.

"Major, this is your ride," said Agent Ray, who had driven us from the airstrip.

"Thanks, Ray. We'll follow." Javi, Dan, and Tom began loading the trunk with our newly acquired equipment and armaments.

"Take a minute to put on the vest, John," said Javi, as he sat in the passenger seat.

"I'll do it when we get to the location. We need to fall in

line here."

I looked for my phone to make sure I had it with me. When I saw the screen it showed five missed calls from Mel. I don't remember hearing the phone ring. Why was Mel calling me?

"John," Javi said, "you want me to drive, man? You seem distracted."

No, I'm cool, bro. Let's go for it and find this tunnel."

About twenty minutes later, we arrived at what seemed to be a city of warehouses and small manufacturing bays. An industrial park, I guessed, was the proper designation for such a place. We were the third vehicle in line. The last two peeled off and looked as if they were going to come in from behind. The lead vehicle with Casselback inside stopped. Agent Ray got out of the front seat and motioned to us to come in through the front door. Everyone moved with stealth and military efficiency. As we walked in, we could see the space was a big open bay with one medium-sized office to the left of the front door. Someone checked the office, and we began walking among all the cases and pallets of boxes from the front to the rear of the structure, as the other two teams came in from the rear and moved towards the front. Within a matter of three or four minutes the entire bay of about four thousand square feet had been searched and cleared. Now we needed to search for the supposed tunnel the waterlogged gang member had told me about back at the Holiday Inn. I swear, if this guy was pulling my leg, he was going to find out what enhanced interrogation was all about. I was getting a feeling I was going to be embarrassed my first day here, and ... somebody shouted, "Here, right here." Everyone moved briskly to the west wall of the warehouse. There, in plain view after removing some pallets filled with boxes of taco shells, was a freaking tunnel. This was not a crude-looking tunnel, like in the movie The Great Escape, although that one had been pretty good. No, no. This was a well-built tunnel, maybe even up to code, with wide steps going down,, and lights and a rail system to move cargo or people more quickly. This had been built to last, and it looked as if had been around for quite a while. We could actually stand and walk without having to crouch down, which made me wonder: What has or who has come through here already? Scary thought to ponder.

Casselback looked around to make sure everyone was there. "Agent Ray, take your team first. Major John, you and your team follow, then Agent Howard and your team. The other two teams stay here."

Before we descended, we took a minute for each of us to put on communication equipment, something we had not done at the Holiday Inn due to the rush to get here.

We had no idea if we were late to the party or early. The freighter had docked two days ago, and the time from the port to here, or Brownsville to be more specific, was about sixteen hours or so away by car according to Google Maps. As we descended into the tunnel, Ray took the lead with his three guys. I followed with Javi, Dan, and Tom. Agent Howard, whom I had not met, brought up the rear with his three guys.

The border was less than a mile from the location of the warehouse. So I expected to have a straight one-mile walk into Mexico.

"John, Howard, this is Ray. Come forward, we have an issue here," Agent Ray said over his COM system. All teams converged at the point where Ray and his team were. We looked in astonishment as the tunnel continued west; however, at this juncture, there were two other tunnels leading into the U.S. side. The one we were following headed east, and then there were two others, one going northeast and the other southeast. Agent Ray said, "John, you and your team keep going west towards Mexico," as he pointed in that direction with his right hand. "Howard, take the tunnel going southeast, and my team, we'll take the tunnel going northeast." Through hand signals to each team, he told them,, "Stay in touch and report anything you see."

"Boys, we are going to Mexico. Please hold off from ordering beers and fajitas until we clear customs. As far as Señoritas ..." I was interrupted, rudely interrupted. "Major, we are all on the COM system; please comment when appropriate only. Thank you," said Special Agent Casselback over the COM system. "Sorry, sir," I replied, looking back at my guys and smiling.

We walked a good mile west. "We must be in Mexico by now," I said. "It still keeps going west. We'll continue." Suddenly we heard what sounded like footsteps. They kept getting a little louder, which meant they were getting closer. No idea who or how many. Could it be the terrorists? All of them making their way now? Or simply a drug run? I motioned by closing my fist for the guys to stop. I crouched down myself and they followed suit. The footsteps stopped. A voice came out of the darkness and asked, "Tequila?" We looked at each other, wondering what that meant. Of course, it was a code that required the appropriate answer.

Javi replied, "Si, tequila."

We heard nothing. About three hours went by. No, maybe half a minute, but it seemed forever. All of a sudden, automatic gunfire opened up, and all I could hear over the incredible loud noise of bullets hitting the walls of the tunnel and the following echo was some crap about a bar. "What the fuck are they saying about a bar? How many are there, you think?" I asked to any one of my guys.

"Sounds like one automatic weapon and one person, John," Javi said.

"Well, they are not all going to shoot at the same time,

are they?"

"Allahu Akbar, Allahu Akbar," said the voice, getting louder as they or he ran towards us. Suddenly, automatic gunfire opened up against us again. I motioned to the guys to fall back. I didn't know what was coming at us. We were all trapped in this tunnel. Four of us against who knows what and how many. Were all twenty terrorists behind this automatic gunfire? How well armed were they? Our fate was sealed if they had grenades or any form of explosives they could send our way. Of course, so was their fate if they made it through us. They would then be trapped in the tunnel. But what fun was that if I was not around to see the end of this encounter? Right?

As we moved back, we knocked out all the light bulbs that had been illuminating the tunnel. Silence and darkness overtook the tunnel. We moved forward quietly about fifty feet from where we had knocked out the lights, giving whoever was there the impression we were further down the tunnel. If it were one or two persons I wanted them alive. We needed the intel. If it were all of them, which I doubted, well, adios amigos. Four of us were not going to stop twenty jihadists.

The rail system ran along one side of the tunnel, which was about eight feet wide, and thus more than half of it was clear for walking, while the other side was for the rail system. This was really well thought out. I whispered to the guys, "Get ready for hand-to-hand." We all took out our knives, and I lay down on the rail system positioning myself to sprint like a tiger. I didn't want to fire shots in such close quarters. Too many chances to hurt ourselves. If it were one or two guys, I expected them to walk by me on the clear path. I did not expect them to be walking on the rails. So, if they walked by me, we would have the element of surprise from two sides. I could hear the footsteps getting closer.

CHAPTER SEVENTEEN

Chicago, Illinois

An open society is a society, which allows its members the greatest possible degree of freedom in pursuing their interests compatible with the interests of others.

—George Soros

Joey called Alex and asked to come to his office to review his findings.

"Mr. C., I've completed my preliminary..." He paused.

"Research," Alex said, finishing the sentence for him.

"Yes, sir, research. I need to share the findings with you."

"Very well, Joey. Come on over."

It was early evening, and the sun was setting over a still Lake Michigan. The mirror effect of the buildings reflecting on the lake was surreal.

Joey walked into Alex's office. "What do you have, Joey?" asked Alex, still enjoying the view of the lake and the sunset before turning around to face Joey.

"Well, I was able to look into a number of items once I had—how should I say it? —opened the files. Yes, opened the files."

"And?" said Alex, pointing to a conference table where Joey could spread his files.

"The Akakios hedge fund seems to do a lot of large trades in its own 'dark pool' account. Trades are constantly going with the market and going against the market."

"That's called going long and short."

"Right. Also, they don't seem to have a lot of clients. Just a handful, the majority of which are offshore accounts whose identities are masked in offshore corporate structures."

"What about Elo Teck, the electronics company that's our client? "Did you see something about them?"

"Here, let me show you," Joey replied, as he opened a file and spread a graph over Alex's desk. "I've mapped news events and/or press releases, and the hedge fund's pattern of trades, one over the other. Normally, you see buyers jump in after good news and sell trades after bad or disappointing news. The Akakios hedge fund seems to be ahead of the trend with this Elo Teck and some other stocks. If you look at the chart, they buy ahead of good news and sell also ahead of bad news. And when I say 'buy' and 'sell,' we are talking millions of dollars worth of trades. They also take advantage of the down trends by selling short and or buying 'puts' on the stocks."

"So," Alex chimed in, "it seems obvious they have some inside information."

"But, if we can see it, can't the Securities and Exchange Commission also see it?" asked Joey.

"Only if they are looking for it. Then, they would ask for an explanation from the hedge fund. More than likely the hedge fund would explain their trading activity and attribute their trades to 'momentum trading,' or something like that."

Joey looked perplexed. "Momentum trading?"

"Simply put, momentum deals with stock volume in one direction or another. Some traders follow the volume and use that as buy or sell signals in trading. When the stock is moving up and there is more volume than normal, the stock is being accumulated. The reverse is also true. Lots of volume on the way down tells you what?"

"The stock is being distributed or dispersed," answered Joey.

"Very good," Alex said, as he sat back in his chair and looked up at the ceiling. "Of course, that has a tendency to exacerbate the volume and becomes a self-fulfilling prophecy as more traders follow the momentum in one direction or the other. Back to Akakios. It would seem they have a system... more than likely an insider trading advantage. Which is exactly what our client was worried about. Someone in our client's company is feeding Akakios or someone in his company with insider information."

"There is more," Joey said.

"On the trades?"

"More on other trades, yes. But there is more about

what you also suspected. Akakios owns an electronics manufacturer in Argentina. From what I have seen, this firm has a proposal ready to go that underbids our client's —Elo Teck— by quite a bit," replied Joey.

"And I bet the hedge fund will be selling the Elo Teck stock and going short as this bid is presented?" suggested Alex rhetorically.

"I also detected a pattern in other trades on stocks and stock indices that doesn't seem to correlate to anything else," Joey said.

"What do you mean?"

"There are nine stocks they are buying and selling daily—big blocks of trades through their dark pool again. Also, they are buying 'puts' on U.S. stock indices and buying 'calls' on the Japan and German stock indices."

"So, they are expecting a correction or drop in the U.S. indices and a bull market movement in Japan and German markets? Interesting. What about the nine companies?"

"Three different sectors. Electronics, three companies; three banks; and three retailers."

Alex's phone rang. His assistant was letting him know that Mr. Akakios's office had called to confirm the appointment for the next day at 3 p.m. Eastern Standard Time in New York City.

"Well, Joey, it looks as if I am going to meet with the mastermind behind all these trades tomorrow. I've been granted an audience with the one and only Mr. Akakios. How about that?"

"What do you hope to gain?"

"An understanding of this guy's mind. He is very reclusive and mysterious. He is also very progressive and liberal to an extreme. His charities mostly deal with organizations united for some form of world transformation. His political action committees—or those he contributes to—are aggressively promoting a left-wing agenda and attacking conservative politicians and/or causes. That's what is of interest to me personally. But I need to feel him out about the possibility of corporate espionage. And I plan to be very direct about that," said Alex, looking at Joey. "Anytime you can meet with someone like this face to face, eye to eye, it can be very revealing. You study the person, his nonverbal communication. And you can gain quite the insight into the person if you are trained to be observant."

"I have a lot to learn."

"You hang around here—around John, Jackie, and me—you can learn very quickly. Right now, I can tell you what you are thinking just by reading your body language."

"Really?"

"Let's see. You are leaning forward; that means you are paying attention and listening with interest to what I am saying. Your arms are to the sides. That tells me you are open to what I'm saying and not rejecting it. Otherwise, your arms would be crossed and you would be leaning back. Also, you have crossed your legs back and forth five times in the last five minutes."

"What does that mean?"

"That, Joey, means you have to go piss really bad but have been patiently listening to me," said Alex, laughing. "Get out of here. You've done good, really good."

"Thank you, Mr. C. You are indeed very perceptive."

CHAPTER EIGHTEEN

Brownsville, Texas

Mexico Border

I was ready to leap on him as one man passed by me in the dark tunnel. I was sure he could hear my heart pounding. The man had to be as nervous as I was. After all, we were surrounded by complete darkness in a small-enclosed tunnel. Everyone was armed and something was about to happen.

A second man was about to pass by me, his right foot really close to the rails where I lay motionless. I could actually smell his feet. My eyes had acclimated to the darkness and I could make out the silhouettes of the two men. Both were holding automatic weapons in front of them. Too dark to tell what they were. They must have assumed that we had retreated back quite a bit. I could tell they were being cautious, but they definitely were not expecting us to be lying on the floor as they walked past us. The question was: How could I jump on this guy without having the other one open fire in the tunnel and put my guys in harm's way? The benefit of working with a teammate in these situations was that after a while you both began to think like the other. I knew Javi was thinking the same as I was. When could we jump them? By now, the first guy had to have reached Javi, as he was lying there on the rails like me. We could easily shoot them both on the spot. But that was not going to get us the intelligence we desperately needed. So, we had to capture both or at least one of them alive. I made the first move, throwing a small rock in the direction from which they came. If the last guy, who was almost on top of me, opened fire to his rear, it would signify that there were only two of them. It was logical to assume he would not shoot if there were more of them following. The first man that passed would be firing with the fear he would hit the guy behind him, but he would turn around and that would allow Javi to jump him.

Sure enough, the man standing next to me turned to open fire behind him. Two quick bursts of automatic gunfire. The sound, again, was deafening. Immediately, I jumped up from my position, now in a crouch, and hit him on the back of his head with the butt of my knife. As I was doing that, I could hear the scuffle behind me. I sure as hell hoped Javi's guy would not open fire, or my guy and me would be toast. My guy fell forward on his knees, still holding his automatic weapon. The burst of fire from his weapon blinded both of us for a moment. What little I could make out of him before was again lost in the darkness. I could feel him in front of me and I needed to disarm him quickly. I grabbed the knife with my left hand and pulled my Glock out with my right hand. In one continuous motion, I smacked the back of his head again... this time with the Glock. He fell forward. I was satisfied he was not going anywhere, and he was going to have a massive headache. I felt around for his rifle and found it underneath him. I could not tell what it was, but it was mine now. I didn't give a shit what it was at this point. He was down and out. No sound came from behind me—which made me feel real good.

"Javi, what's up?"

"We are good, John. We have this guy down and under control."

"I think this is it. Dan, Tom, please cover our rear. We'll start back with these two hombres."

"You got it, John," said Dan, walking past John, with Tom following.

Tom whispered, "Cut your communication device. Dan and Javi have already done it."

Tom waited and said, "You realize if we go back the FBI is going to take these two and start questioning them. Maybe even read them their rights, right?"

We started walking back towards the Mexico side of the tunnel where there were still lights attached to their sockets. "So what you are saying is that we should do the questioning while we are still in Mexico, correct?" John said.

"Time is of the essence, John. We have two of twenty, brother. We are not government and we are still on the

Mexico side. Like you say, John, go for it," Tom said.

"This is not going to be easy. These guys are looking forward to their virgins. They may be ready to commit suicide on this mission. How the hell do you question them so they give up something?" Javi asked.

"That's going to be a problem going forward in this war against terrorism. If our enemy is Islamic radicalism, then we had better understand their culture, religion, and motivation. Otherwise, it's going to be like trying to fix a computer with a screwdriver and a hammer," I said, looking at Javi. "Let's go back. We have limited resources here to question these two. We've done our job. Let the experts take over."

Tying our captives' hands behind their backs, we started walking back to the entrance of the tunnel. Dan led in front, followed by Javi and his prisoner, then me and my prisoner, and finally Tom brought up the rear.

"Special agent, this is John Powers. We are on our way back with two prisoners," I said, after turning on our COM system.

"Great job, John. We lost you there for a moment. Is everyone in one piece?"

"Everyone including the new arrivals, sir. There are eighteen others going somewhere else." I made no comment about our COM system being off for a bit.

"I hear you, John. Bring these guys back. Let's see what

intel we can get from them."

"Roger that. Back in a few minutes." As much as I wanted to interrogate these two, I had no way of doing it. Short of using my knife to start cutting things off, what could I do? I really had a bad feeling about these incursions into the U.S. We stopped two of them. What about the others? Where were they going and why?

CHAPTER NINETEEN

Mexico City

They finally gathered all their belongings and met Antonio, their driver, at the entrance to the hotel where he had been waiting with his Honda Odyssey van. Antonio was a jovial sixty-plus fellow from Merida, Mexico. It was a little after midday in Mexico City, and Julia had completed her meeting. She was now ready for a little relaxation and an outing with Jackie and Mel prior to flying back to Chicago tomorrow as planned. Before they checked out of the Presidente Hotel, Julia had been able to call home but only spoke to Alex's assistant, Joy. Julia told her everything was fine and she would call Alex later from their new hotel.

Antonio drove out of the city and made his way to Route 95, heading south to Cuernavaca. After about forty minutes, they were out of the city and entering areas of sparse population near Tlalpan, Mexico.

All three ladies were looking forward to their stay at Las Mañanitas Hotel in Cuernavaca—a quaint location, a beautiful setting, and great food. Many nice places in Mexico, Julia had been told by Alex, are usually enclosed by tall walls, with a Mexico B outside and a Mexico A inside the walls. Julia had already noticed this: There was poverty, dirty streets, and homeless people walking around areas of the city that seemed almost abandoned. Then once the destination was reached, passing through a security gate in the walled compound revealed a paradise of foliage, flowers, and cleanliness, with well-kept properties, usually a hotel, restaurant, private club, or other establishment. That was Mexico A, and the contrast could not be more distinct.

"*Señoritas*, there seems to be an accident up ahead. We have local police conducting traffic," he said.

"Anything to be concerned about, Antonio?" Jackie asked, concerned but not alarmed.

"No, this happens many times," he replied.

As they approached the scene, they could see a blue van on the side of the road and a police car that was partially blocking their passage. Two policemen waved them forward and motioned to Antonio to stop. One policeman smiled as he signaled for Antonio to roll down his window, while the second made his way to the other side of the car.

"Hay un problema," the policeman said through Antonio's open window.

"There's a problem," Jackie repeated to Mel, who was sitting on the passenger side of the van.

Antonio got out of the car as he unlocked all doors.

Immediately, the policeman by the driver's side door drew his pistol and got in the car, while in the same split second, the second policeman rolled open the back sliding door of the van, with his gun drawn and pointing it at Julia and Jackie.

Mel still had her bag strapped over her shoulder and, putting her hand in the bag, she cautiously clutched her Glock 19.

"Ladies," the policeman in the front said in broken English, "there is change of plans. Please come out of the car and go to blue car." He motioned with his pistol to the direction he wanted them to take. "Everything is OK."

As they were getting out of Antonio's van, three other men got out of the blue van, and one opened the side door for them.

"Don't do anything stupid," said Jackie.

"That is a good thing, miss," said the policeman.

As Julia and Jackie were getting into the van, Mel faked a fall and rolled off into a small embankment on the side of the road. The men pushed Julia and Jackie inside the van, as a fourth man placed a bag over each of their heads. The men quickly boarded the blue van and began to take off.

"¿Que hago con la flaca?" said the policeman to the men in the blue van.

"The skinny one is yours. We have what we want. Do what you like," said the driver of the van, laughing as he sped off in a southerly direction.

The policemen, holding their pistols, looked carefully

as they began going down the embankment, slipping and sliding with the rocks.

"*Señor*, my ankle is broken," Mel said. She had positioned herself so she could look up at the road with her right hand still inside her knit bag with the Glock 19 at the ready. As the two policemen were getting close, Mel noticed both had put their pistols away, not sensing any danger from this young lady who appeared hurt. Raising her right hand, she slowly squeezed the trigger four times, hitting the center mass of both policemen in the chest, twice each. She saw their surprised look as both fell to their knees right in front of her. She rolled to her right to avoid being struck by one of them falling forward onto her.

"Antonio!" she screamed, looking around for the driver as she got up from the dirt. "Antonio," she called out again. As she made it up to the road, she saw that Antonio's van was still there next to the now empty police car. Looking around, she saw a figure running down the opposite embankment. "Antonio!" she called out again. She fired her Glock one time into the air. Antonio looked back. She could see the fear in his eyes. He was about fifty yards away and moving fast through the bushes. All that was ahead was open field. She reached into the van and grabbed the keys before quickly putting her Glock away and breaking into a dash after Antonio. "You're not getting away, prick," she said out loud.

With her long legs she ran like a gazelle, making ground on Antonio who seemed to be slowing down and getting out of breath. Antonio tripped and fell on his face as Mel was but ten yards from him. "Stay down, you son of a bitch," she said, as she pulled out her Glock. Antonio was gasping for air. He extended his arms outward to show he was unarmed and was no threat. "Turn around, facing up," she demanded.

"*Señorita*, I didn't do anything. I think the police were going to kill me, so I ran," he said as he tried to catch his breath.

"Look, I don't have much time for bullshit. Answer two questions or you are going to be in a lot of pain. *¿Entiendes, amigo?* Who took my friends? And where are they taking them?" she asked, pointing the gun at Antonio.

"I don't know. Please, believe me," he said.

"Listen carefully. I have ten rounds left on my gun. I will use nine on your hands, knees, feet, shoulders, one on your fat belly, and the last on your forehead. Answer my fucking questions," she screamed.

"They will kill me," he said desperately.

"Not after I kill you first here and leave your body to rot. Answer! Who and where?"

Antonio hesitated.

With Antonio on the ground facing up, Mel moved her Glock close to his left hand, aimed and pulled the trigger.

The echo of the shot could be heard in the open field that was otherwise quiet.

"*Chingada*, you shot me, why?" shouted Antonio, as he grabbed his left hand with his right while still lying face up on the ground.

She took his right hand and moved the barrel of her gun, this time aiming at his right hand, and said, "Antonio?"

"The Jimenez cartel. I don't know where. Believe me," he said loudly in pain.

Mel turned around and began to sprint back to the van. As she got inside, she pulled the keys out of her pocket, started the engine, made a U-turn and began driving back to what she hoped would be Mexico City. She had no clue. She pulled out her phone and dialed Alex's cell phone. The phone rang and a recorded message said, *"Aviso de metrocell, su llamada no puede ser comunicada, favor de..."* "Fuck you," she said in a desperate voice and hung up. She drove, looking for a sign to Mexico City.

CHAPTER TWENTY

Brownsville, Texas

We had captured two of the suspected twenty men posing as Mexicans who planned to illegally enter the U.S. Unlike most of the normal illegal immigrants who risk all to come to the United States for an opportunity at a better life, these men had a different objective.

They were not coming to the U.S. to better their lives. No, they were coming to the U.S. to end some of our lives. Questioning by the FBI and the other agents involved in this mission did not result in any viable intelligence. Both men refused to say anything. They knew we knew they were not Mexicans. That was made very clear when one of them had shouted *"Allahu Akbar"* in the tunnel as he rushed us with his automatic weapon. I guess if he had shouted *"Quiero Chimichangas,"* he maybe would have passed as a Mexican for a little longer, but not much longer. Shit, I wanted an opportunity to take one of these guys to the shower as I had done with the gang member.

Last night we were thanked for capturing the two men and then told to get some food and let them do their thing with these two. Javi found a Tex-Mex restaurant called El Sol Caliente or The Hot Sun, and we had showered and gone there. We had a great dinner with a few – well, maybe more than a few – *cervesas Mejicanas*. My hope was that we would get a call during dinner with directions to go elsewhere as a result of the questioning. But no such luck. The more time passed, the better the chance for the remaining eighteen men to achieve their goal and enter the U.S. Worse than that, once in, they were going to very hard to track.

I walked over to where Special Agent Casselback was. “Sir, may I speak with you privately?” He looked at me a little funny, but hey, we had apprehended these two without firing one shot ourselves and brought them back in one piece, so he owed us that.

“Yes, John, what’s on your mind?” he said, as we walked out of the makeshift command center and stepped into the parking lot outside.

“Sir, we don’t have much time. These guys are spreading out as we speak, and we are sitting here playing with our ...” Well, I didn’t finish the thought.

“John, we’ve tried almost everything on these two.”

“The key word is ‘almost,’ from what I hear. Allow me to question one of these men with my team.”

“John...”

“Sir, the gang member was not hurt when we questioned him. The end result was valuable information that led us to the tunnel.” I liked this guy, but what the fuck was he waiting for? Of course, I said that to myself.

He looked at me without saying a word. He started to walk back to the command center with me trailing him.

"Agent," he said to one of the guards, "take Major Powers to the room of one of the captured men. He needs to ask some questions." He looked back at me.

"David, I need my team with me."

"Very well, do it."

I got hold of Javi, Dan, and Tom. When we got to the room we dismissed the two guards in front of the door and the one guard inside the room. They hesitated, but the agent accompanying us nodded to them and they quietly left the area. As we walked into the room we noticed the difference between this room and the one where the gang member was being held. This room had nothing in it except a mattress on the floor. No sheets, no pillows, nothing. The man had been handcuffed and leg cuffed. He was free to move around the room, I guess. He was sitting on the floor by his bed. He had been given a prayer rug and a Koran. The moment the four of us walked in, his expression changed with anticipation and fear. I was glad it did. I wanted to make sure he knew we were there for business, not square dancing. Javi spoke Spanish to him. This guy was fluent in Spanish. It was quite the training they had received in Cuba. They were on a serious mission to go to that length. I could hear Javi being the good cop and asking nicely, as I am sure the prior questioning had gone. This guy must think we were a bunch of patsies. As with the gang member, I became slowly irritated as this man looked at me, and then at Javi as I paced back and forth behind him, all the while looking with evil intentions at the prisoner. "No more bullshit," I said out loud, reaching for the man's shirt and pulling him up to a standing position. His eyes almost popped out as I did that. I put my face right in front of his, one inch apart, and screamed, "What is your mission?" I was too close to see, but the man jumped a foot off the floor as I screamed into his face, Javi told me later. I got no response, and with that I yanked the man into the bathroom and into the tub.

My phone kept vibrating but I paid no attention to it. It was inside my pocket, and I had no time to answer it. For an hour I shower-boarded this fucking guy until we finally got something from him. Dollars to doughnuts, these guys have gone through this experience as part of their training. It worked, because we broke his resistance to it after an hour. Shit, after an hour of his thinking he was going to drown over and over, it got a bit arduous for him to resist.

I went back to Casselback. As I walked into the conference room, which served as our command center, everyone turned to look at me with great anticipation. Evidently, Casselback had let them in on the secret that my team was talking to one of them. The room was now totally quiet. I looked around the room, smiled, and announced,

"This guy and his partner finally admitted that"—I paused for dramatic effect—"that they will not eat *carnitas*." I thought it was funny; you see *carnitas* were pork-filled fajitas, but half the room was giving me the middle finger mentally, as the other half smiled. Only one person, some computer geek, laughed out loud, and he quickly seemed totally embarrassed. Shit, so much for my stand-up comedy act in Brownsville. These stiff necks had no sense of humor. "Actually, while I have your attention – and thank you for that – their targets are malls, shopping malls." This got their attention. Casselback waved me over to his table where he stood with the other guys, looking at a map of the border with possible entry points marked along it.

"So, John, he admitted to going after shopping malls?" asked the special agent.

"He said that his target is a shopping mall in Corpus Christi. He does not know if the others also have malls as their targets. He and his partner were headed to a safe house in Corpus Christi. I guess the others have safe houses, too. They were to wait there for instructions on when to begin. The plan was to set off a series of bombs in the mall and detonate them in a sequence so as to maximize the number of casualties and terror. Each team of two received individual instructions so as to minimize exposure of the plan should anyone be captured."

"Can we plant our own men instead of these two, and

have them follow the plan until they get to the house?" asked one of the men around the table.

"Good question," I replied. "Except they were supposed to check in yesterday, as they crossed the border. So, no, they already know we got these two."

"You think they may move the attack forward then?" asked another of the men.

Casselback replied, "No, I think there is a particular date they have in mind. If the information each team has is compartmentalized, as it seems to be, then they have nothing to worry about. They have ten teams; they can afford to lose one, two, three. Remember, these assholes only have to be right once."

My phone vibrated again. I saw it was Mel, whom I guessed was still in Mexico with Jackie and Ms. Julia. I put the phone back in my pocket so we could finish this discussion.

"It makes sense that everyone will have different types of targets, don't you think?" I asked no one in particular.

"Why do you say that?" someone asked.

"Well, if we capture a team, as we have, and are able to pull information out as we did, and all targets are shopping malls, then we are going to act on it and protect malls," I said.

"You know how many malls there are?" another person asked.

"Yes. But, it would make better sense if the targets were altogether different. Don't you agree, sir?" I addressed Casselback directly. I didn't want everyone around the table giving an opinion.

"Makes sense, John. However, unless we capture a second team, we will not know for sure. I want to send a team to Corpus Christi to look around. Did we get a name of a specific mall?"

"We did not, sir," I replied. "I believed him when he said he did not know at this point."

"Okay. Ray, put a team of four together and send them over to Corpus Christi," Casselback said to Agent Ray and added, "Our work is not done, and as a matter of fact, it just started. Let's continue our efforts to locate other entry points."

I started back to meet with my guys. The guys from Homeland and the CIA were all scurrying out to expedite the report. Finally, I had a minute so I took out my phone and realized that Mel had called eleven times. I quickly called her back.

"What's up, young lady?" I asked as she answered the phone.

"John, I've called a million times. I've got bad news, and I have not spoken to Alex or you," she said in a semi-frantic tone. "Julia and Jackie have been kidnapped."

I could not believe what she had just said. "Say what,

Mel? Julia and Jackie have been kidnapped?" I asked, hoping I had not heard correctly.

"Yes, John. The Jimenez cartel kidnapped them on our way to Cuernavaca. I was able to escape, and they had no interest in kidnapping me. They were assisted by the local police, and our driver was in on it."

"How do you know this?" I asked, still incredulous about the news I was hearing.

"I dealt with the police in a terminal way, if I make myself clear. Then, I questioned the driver somewhat forcefully. He admitted to helping the cartel but had no clue as to where they were taking them."

"And you believe him?"

"Yes, I do," she replied. "I am driving back to Mexico City, following the road and the signs. Have no clue what to do next."

"You have money?"

"Yes, why?"

"Drive as far as you can into the city. Ditch the car you are in, and take a taxi to a hotel."

"Should I go back to where we were staying, the Presidente Hotel?"

"No, don't do that. If they come looking, that will be the first place they will look."

"Understood. I'll find a small hotel and call you as soon as I do. Are you going to call Alex?" she asked me. It hit me that Alex had no clue about all that had transpired, and I was going to have to break the news to him.

"Mel, take care of yourself. I'll call Alex. You call me the moment you check in." Shit, breaking the news to Alex was not going to be easy. I had no idea what to expect.

CHAPTER TWENTY-ONE
Cuernavaca, Mexico

The four who had kidnapped Julia and Jackie had received strict orders not to touch Julia. Jackie, however, was a wanted person by the Jimenez cartel, and there were no restrictions as to what they could do to her, except that both of them were to be alive for their trip to Cuba. Both Julia and Jackie had their heads covered with a canvas bag and their hands were tied behind their backs. Julia sat in the second row of seats in the van with one man beside her; Jackie was in the third row with two of the four men sitting beside her. They had removed her clothing, except for her panties. Each took his turn fondling her, kissing her breasts, belly button, neck, and lower body. At first she had resisted...she screamed, and kicked, only to be slapped and have her legs restrained with a rope. The man with Julia switched places with one in the third row, so he too could have his fun with Jackie. Neither Julia nor Jackie could see the men's faces or their gang tattoos all over their arms and necks. Had they been able to actually see these men, they would have been petrified – not that they were not scared as it was.

"Why can't we touch *la guera esta*?" asked one of the men.

"We have orders not to touch the blonde woman, so don't," said the driver to the man in the second row with Julia. "The other one worked for us at one time."

"What do you mean for us? For Jimenez?" asked the man in the second row.

"*Sí, manito.* She worked for us. She was a pilot for Jimenez. Then later we found out she was DEA," said the driver. "Señor Jimenez wants her."

Jackie cried out from the back seat, *"No mas, hijos de puta, no mas."*

Upon hearing that, Julia chimed in. "Stop whatever you are doing, please stop."

The two men with Jackie laughed as one of them slapped her again through the canvas bag covering her head.

The driver said, "Put her clothes on. We are getting close to the airport."

"Why?" said one of the men, laughing. "They are going to take them off in the plane anyway."

"Just do as I say. Do it now, *cabron,*" ordered the driver.

The van was about one mile from the General Mariano Matamoros Airport. A government-owned agency operated the airport and had a small annual passenger count. Most of the traffic was of a local nature in and around Cuernavaca. This time, however, an international flight was waiting to take off. Cuban Directorate of Intelligence agents were waiting to whisk Julia and Jackie direct to Varadero Beach, Cuba, where Colonel Abimbola awaited their arrival with great anticipation. A Fairchild-Dornier 328JET was gassed and waiting with its engines running as the van made its entrance to the airport and proceeded to the runway where the jet was expecting their arrival. The distance between Cuernavaca and Varadero Beach, Cuba, was a great circle distance of 1,195 miles. A great circle is the shortest distance between two points on a sphere. The flight time would be a bit under three hours since the 328JET had a cruising speed of about 466 miles per hour. Their destination in Cuba was the Kawama Airport, also with only one runway. Interestingly, this particular 328JET was one of two left in Cuba from an original fleet of eight planes owned by MonteCarlo Industries in Miami, the same company that Julia Muller had worked to take public on the New York Stock Exchange in 2000 until the United States government had intervened to prevent it from doing so. The FBI proved the company was really owned by the Cuban government and the stock offering was a sham to launder ten billion dollars of illicit gains under what the Castro brothers had named Operation Due Diligence. The failure of that operation was the main motivation for Colonel Abimbola to get even with Alex Cardenas and Jackie Allison. Julia was the bait and a welcome enhancement for his revenge.

"Where are you taking us?" asked Julia, as she was being taken out of the van, still with her head covered.

"Don't worry, *Señora*. You are going to one of the most beautiful beaches in the world," said Raul, the driver of the van. "I hope you brought your swimsuits."

The other three men laughed, as they pulled Jackie out of the van and walked her, together with Julia, up the steps to the door of the plane. As Julia and Jackie were assisted into the plane, one of the men was showing the others the photos of Jackie that he had taken with his cell phone as he had had his fun with her in the van. They laughed as the agent inside the plane closed the door. They walked down the steps and headed to their van.

Julia and Jackie were assisted to their seats and their head covers were removed. Both had been sweating profusely from the bags over their heads and they were given small hand towels and bottles of water to drink. Their hands were untied and they were allowed to sit uncovered and unbound in the plane.

Julia again said, "I demand to know where you are taking us."

The agents looked at each other and smiled as one of them said, "Miss Julia, you and your companion, Miss Jackie, have a date with Colonel Abimbola in Cuba. He has questions for both of you and is looking forward to having Mr. Alex visit with us in Varadero Beach."

"You are kidnapping us and taking us to Cuba?" asked Julia in a rhetorical manner. "Do you realize that we are American citizens?"

"No, Miss Julia. Not kidnapping. We are taking you for a visit. You were born in Cuba, so as far as we know, you are a Cuban citizen first," replied the agent, who seemed to be the boss. A man of about forty years old, he had small beady eyes, a sharp pointed nose, and a lipless mouth with the top of it covered by a mustache.

Julia looked at Jackie, assessing their situation. Jackie was still recovering from the ride in the van where the three Mexican cartel members had subjected her to humiliating acts. She was in no mood to talk or to challenge these Cuban men. She was resigned to whatever came at this point.

"Who is Colonel Abimbola? And why is he waiting for us?" asked Julia, as she sat back in her seat after drying herself off and drinking some water.

"Colonel Abimbola will soon explain everything to you. Just remember that the two of you and Cardenas are responsible for the failure of MonteCarlo Industries and for Mr. Rick Ramirez being in a U.S. jail right now," said the agent, looking at Julia.

"I don't think they are taking us there to go to the beach, Julia," said Jackie, recovering from her ordeal.

"I know," said Julia, as she put her head down.

CHAPTER TWENTY-TWO

Brownsville, Texas

Prior to calling Alex, I met with Casselback and brought him up to date on my situation. I told him I could leave Dan and Tom behind. However, Javi was coming with me. We were getting ready to head down to Mexico City and meet up with Melissa.

"Shit, man, I wish I could do more for you guys," said Casselback, really meaning it. "But I got a situation here ..."

I interrupted, "David, no need to apologize. We all understand perfectly. You can't go where we are going anyway. I wish we could stay and follow through on this mission with you." Making my way out of the door, I noticed Javi had secured some equipment. We made sure not to bring any weapons with us, as Mexico's laws were quite strict about that for foreigners. I wished they had strict laws about kidnappings and drug dealing for their own people. I called Alex. "Alex, I am afraid I have some very bad news." Without hesitating, I continued, "Julia and Jackie have been kidnapped on their way to Cuernavaca" – not taking a breath, I kept speaking– "Javi and I are on our way to meet up with Mel in Mexico City. Mel witnessed everything and even shot two policemen who were accomplices in the kidnapping." There was silence for what seemed a long minute. I could tell Alex was both thinking and wanting to scream at the same time.

Alex finally spoke in a controlled voice, "Who did this? Does Mel know?"

"According to their car driver whom Mel forced to speak up, it was the Jimenez cartel gang members. But no one knew where they were headed."

"Fuck. The only connection with the Jimenez cartel is Jackie. She worked for them in tandem with her husband, as pilots while she was with the DEA. I hope ..."

His voice just trailed off before finishing his sentence. "Alex, meet us in Mexico City. We'll pick up Mel and begin to follow whatever trail we can get. If we have to ask every fucking gang member of this cartel, we will. They are not going to hurt either Julia or Jackie, my friend."

"Very well, John. I am on my way. We'll connect by phone if anything develops. I must tell you, I've been having this bad feeling in my stomach since Julia left."

"Alex, we are going to need weapons once we are in Mexico." I didn't want to discuss the situation so I kept it short and business-like. Feeling like shit, I realized that on my end I had a deep concern for Jackie beyond just the usual co-worker concern.

"Understood. I'll arrange for that and transportation. Get your ass and Javi's to the city. And, John, thank you."

"Brother, be assured that this will be a successful operation. I'll see you soon."

That was harder than I thought. Alex really held it together. I know inside he must be dying with a million things going around in his head.

As we were getting ready to leave Agent Ray came over to where we were standing. At first I thought he just wanted to say his good-byes.

"Major, hang on a second before you take off," he said, as he hurried over to us.

"Ray, we are in a hurry. Time is of the essence here."

"We understand it is. Special Agent Casselback has instructed our pilots to take you wherever you need to go to. The Gulfstream you came here from Chicago in is at your disposal for a one-way flight. That is, if you want it."

"If we want it? Are you fucking kidding me? That is really great of Special Agent Casselback."

"Just be gone. The plane is waiting and ready to go," said Agent Ray, smiling.

"Ray, please thank the special agent. I am sure Alex will be in his debt." Shit, this was exactly what we needed at the moment, a quick and quiet ride to Mexico City.

CHAPTER TWENTY-THREE

Chicago, Illinois

"Joy, cancel all my appointments today and get me a ticket to Mexico City. Better yet, please come in here a second," said Alex over the intercom to his assistant. His voice was trembling a bit.

Joy came in quickly as she noticed Alex's concern in his voice when he spoke. "Yes, sir, what is it you need me to do?"

"I am afraid there is bad news, but I want it contained to just those that need to know. Julia and Jackie have been kidnapped in Mexico," he said, covering his face with both hands and almost gasping for air.

"Oh, my Lord," Joy replied. "I'll get you a flight out to Mexico City immediately. What about Mel?"

"She seems to have escaped the kidnapping. We need to call Andy upstairs and bring him up to date. Better yet, have him come down and tell him immediately. I'll tell him, if I am here. Otherwise, you tell him."

"What is the plan?"

"John and Javi are on their way to Mexico City to meet up with Mel. They plan to retrace the steps they took before the kidnapping. Unfortunately, Mel took permanent action against two guys who could have had more information and supposedly got as much out of another as possible."

"Well, if they kidnapped for money, we should be hearing something soon. Don't you think?"

"I have a feeling, Joy, that this goes beyond that. The gang that took them is affiliated with the Jimenez cartel. And, you don't know this, but, Jackie was undercover with the DEA and embedded in the Jimenez cartel back before 2000."

"Oh, boy! Let me call Andy. I will also cancel your flight to New York and your appointment with Mr. Akakios."

"Forgot about him. Yes, do that, but don't tell anyone any specifics. Shit! I had a feeling."

"Don't beat yourself up, sir. There was no way you could have prevented this from happening. You've got good people working on it,' said Joy, as she walked out of the room.

"Have Joey begin an immediate research of the Jimenez cartel and any related gang activity associated with them. I doubt they have a website, the cartel that is, but tell him to do his magic and research everything," said Alex, as Joy was walking out of his office.

Andy Anderson came down from his office upstairs. Alex thought that, as Julia's partner, Andy had lived through the anguish of her attempted assassination by the Cuban government in 2000, and the sorrow she had suffered while married to her now deceased husband, Dr. Jonathan Muller. He did not know how much more Julia could take, and he worried how much Andy could personally take. Alex explained everything to him, as he got ready to depart to the airport.

Alex's personal line rang in his office. He looked at the phone and looked outside to Joy's desk to see if she would pick up. He didn't want to take any calls right now. Joy answered the call.

"Alex," she said, addressing him by his first name, which she never did. "There is a Colonel Abimbola on the line for you, sir.

Alex looked at her with a quizzical expression on his face. He raised his eyebrows, as if asking who the hell is that? Joy got the hint and inquired of the caller.

"May I ask, Colonel, what this is about?" she said as Alex moved next to her to listen in.

Colonel Abimbola replied, "*Sí*, please tell him that I am having a very pleasant chat with his fiancée."

Alex quickly went back to his office, closing his door. As he did, he motioned to Andy to take a seat, picking up the phone. "You son of a bitch, what do you think you are doing?"

"Alejandro, please don't be so rude. You know we Cubans take an insult to our mother very, very seriously. So, I advise you to be civil, and let's have a conversation. *¿Sí,* *amigo?"* said the colonel.

"What do you want?" Alex asked, holding back an intense fury that he could not unleash over the phone.

"Ah, that's more like it. See, you can be Cuban and have a civil conversation at the same time. Let me get to the point. I know you are a busy man. I want a simple trade. Your Julia for you, even up."

"Where is Julia's companion?"

"Oh, the beautiful Jackie Allison, DEA agent extraordinaire. Yes, she is here also. Jimenez wanted her to stay in Mexico, but I said, no, we need to keep the ladies together. After all, I may need her for pictures I would like to send to Rick Ramirez. He misses his lover and confidante. Right, Mr. Cardenas? So, what is it going to be? You, for Julia? Or, did the CIA remove your testicles when you retired from the agency?" the colonel asked in a taunting tone.

Alex raised his gaze to Andy who was sitting across from Alex's desk. Andy was pale as a sheet, his face drained completely of color. Alex felt like throwing up. He wanted to grab this prick's neck and pull him through the phone lines.

"What is your fucking name again? Arringola?"

"No, Mr. Cardenas, my first name is Abimbola. It means 'born-rich' in African. You seem to be losing your cool. I am holding all the cards in this game, so I implore you to be civil and don't jeopardize any opportunity to save your fiancée."

"So, what do you want?" asked Alex, visibly upset and distracted.

"Like I said before, it's very simple. You for Julia Muller. That simple. Fly in at your leisure to Varadero Beach Airport. Once there, call me. I'll have you picked up and we can make the exchange. How does that sound?"

Alex was speechless. The colonel was in total control of the situation. Alex could hear his heart beating loudly and could feel that his face was flushed and hot.

"Mr. Cardenas, while you think about it, here's a little trivia for you. Varadero Airport was the first airport to accommodate a hijacked jet plane to Cuba in 1960. Our airport in Havana was not long enough to have a jet land there."

"Very well. I want both Julia Muller and Jackie Allison in exchange for me ..."

Abimbola did not let him finish. "Hang on. I said Julia Muller. Miss Allison may want to stay here, after we show her our love for her, over and over," the colonel said, laughing.

"Colonel, both ladies have to be in perfect condition, and both are to come back to the U.S., after I land in Varadero. You got that?"

"Alex, Alex, you have no leverage here. You can't demand shit," the colonel said, raising his voice. "Got that, amigo? If Miss Jackie wants to leave us, so be it. Miss Julia has not been touched. Can't say the same thing about Jackie, but I'll have both ready for you."

"We'll do the exchange at the airport when I land."

"Excellent. Say, two days from now?"

"I want to speak to both of them right now."

"Hang on." It took the colonel a few minutes to walk to the location where Julia was being held.

"Hello? Alex?" asked Julia, as the colonel handed over the phone.

"Oh, my God, Julia. Are you all right?"

"Yes, my love, I am fine. I am sorry ..."

Alex interrupted. "Is Jackie with you?"

The colonel grabbed the phone away from Julia. "There, Alex, you've spoken to your fiancée, and she claims to be all right. She is here in Varadero. Just show up in two days and she goes back to the U.S.A. *¿Entiende?"*

"I'll be there in two days," replied Alex in a resigned manner as he hung up the phone. He sat back in his chair, tilting his head back and looking at the ceiling in his office. He closed his eyes and rubbed his face with both hands.

Andy, who had been sitting there in total amazement at the entire conversation, got up from his chair across from Alex and served him a cold glass of water from a thermos that was next to the desk. "Are you OK?" he asked.

"I'll be fine, Andy. Let me catch my breath. Thank you

for the water."

"What are you going to do?" asked Andy.

"One, I am going to Cuba. Two, I am getting both Julia and Jackie out. And three, I am killing this bastard. Andy, don't feel bad, but I need some privacy to plan this. Do you mind?"

"No need to ask, please. I'll get out of the way. I think we should keep this private. On a need-to-know basis, don't you agree?"

"By all means. Keep your office in the dark and I'll do the same here. I think it is best right now."

Alex got his composure back and began formulating a plan. He was back in the game. Planning.

"Joy, get Joey up here," Alex said and reached for his phone to call John, who was in-flight to Mexico City.

CHAPTER TWENTY-FOUR

At 40,000 Feet Altitude

"This plane is really comfortable," I mentioned to Javi who was sitting across from me in this beautiful Gulfstream. Unfortunately, we were not on a pleasure ride or on our way to a vacation. My sat phone rang. "This is John Powers," I answered.

"John, where are you now?" I could tell from his voice that Alex was still very – what's the word? Emotional? Nervous?

Replying, I said, "Yes, Boss, we are about one hour away from landing in Mexico City. What's up?" I was hoping he did not have any more bad news. What we knew was bad enough, right?

"Julia and Jackie are in Cuba."

"Cuba?" I was totally not expecting this turn of events. "Why Cuba, and how do you know?

"It seems there is a revenge factor involved here. I got a call from a colonel in the Cuban intelligence service that wants to trade Julia for me."

"Hang on. What about Jackie?"

"I agreed to be traded for both Julia and Jackie. He wants me to fly into Varadero Airport, east of Havana about ninety miles. I am to be there in two days, and we will make the exchange on the tarmac. I stay; they board and come back."

"That isn't gonna fucking happen, Boss," I said. Javi was looking at me with a "what the fuck is going on?" expression on his face.

"Of course not, John. Call Mel. Have her meet you at the airport in Mexico City. I am going to make a few calls, so we can keep the plane a little longer. I heard from Casselback and he told me you have the Gulfstream."

"I don't think we should fly into Cuba with a CIA plane. That could complicate things a bit. I have an idea, Alex."

"I'm all ears," he replied.

My mind was going at full speed. I guess Joey would say my CPU was processing at warp speed, or something like that. "We need Joey to do some research and see if he can pinpoint the exact location in Varadero where this colonel is."

"I'm ahead of you there. I've had Julia's computer brought to the office. It seems these people have hacked into it and probably into our systems. So, I am hoping Joey can reverse the procedure and hack back, I guess I'll call it. Varadero is not your typical place to hold prisoners or hostages. It's a beach for tourists and the Cuban elite."

Great minds think alike. I said to myself. However, I didn't think Alex would appreciate levity at this moment. "See if we can get clearance to fly into Homestead Air Force

Base in Homestead, Florida. That's going to put us about an hour's driving time from Islamorada, Florida."

"And what's there, John?"

"Boss, I have an older brother, Captain James, who has a great fishing charter business out of World Wide Sportsman Bayside Marina. Anyway, he has a kickass boat. That's our ticket to Varadero Beach," I said excitedly. I knew we could not fly in, so the next best thing was to take a boat under cover of night and make our way into town.

"Very well, John. I like the idea. I'll call about the plane and the air force base landing. You call Mel and your brother. Is he going to be willing to take us to Cuba?"

"He is my older brother, but he is only a captain. Fuck, I am a major. He'll be more than willing to go on this mission. He's always been a little envious of my Delta Force days and other spy shit. Now he can be part of a mission. If not, we'll leave his ass on the dock and take his boat anyway. Count on it, Boss." Of course, it was me that was envious of Big Bro James, living in the Keys, fishing everyday, relaxing in a laid-back casual lifestyle, drinking cold cervesas —a real Conch Republic existence. Chasing tunas and dolphins instead of bad guys was a much better alternative. Tunas and dolphins don't shoot back. Just the fact that I wouldn't have to wear long pants, shoes, and a gun everyday would be motivation enough for me. Maybe I'll get me a boat and hang with Bro after this.

"See you at Homestead. I am sure after my calls they will contact your pilot and arrange for the second leg of your flight. I hope they have a second movie for you to watch," Alex said.

I could detect a little smile coming from Alex. Seeing that a plan was forming made him feel better, I was sure. My thoughts immediately turned to Jackie. Shit, she was the one who had brought the whole thing down for the Cuban generals and ended plans for the offering of the Miami company going public on the New York Stock Exchange. She was embedded as the lover of Ramirez, the CEO for MonteCarlo Industries, and was privy to all their dealings. Ramirez had trusted her. Of course, that had been the DEA's plan... start with a single Latin lover, who was rich, arrogant, and loves toys, and put that together with an attractive young bombshell, a pilot for a drug cartel who was willing to play, and you had a perfect situation. The fact that she spilled the beans on them worried me that they were willing to let her go so easy. I explained to Javi who was in total bewilderment sitting there listening to the conversation about what was going on. I brought him up to date and asked him to call Mel while I called Big Bro.

"Big Bro Jaime, what's up, man?" I said, as my brother picked up the phone.

"Little shit Johnny, what are you doing calling me? You need someone to clean your behind?"

We laughed. We shared a mom, as we had different fathers. But we were raised together until I enlisted in the Army and he went to school. Different last names, but we shared the same hard-core healthy principles, inherited or better yet, instilled in us by our mom. Come to think of it, she loved her beer, too, as much as we did. Last time we spoke was after some storm went through the Keys, and we had not connected since. He did his shit, and I did mine. That was how it was.

"How come you are not fishing, brother, or are you?"

"One of those rare days here when we get some bad rainstorms. Had to cancel a charter this morning. What can I do for you?"

"Captain, I have job for you. It may involve some risk."

"Some of your spy stuff?" he asked.

"Well, I am privately employed and no longer associated with the government. But, yes, it's a little spy stuff, I guess. Are you in?"

"What do you need, Major?"

"How long would it take to reach Varadero Beach in Cuba from your dock?"

"I have to do some work with my charts and the computer, so off the top of my head, about five or so hours. Why?"

"Captain, you are picking up a charter to go to Cuba either tonight or tomorrow night. We need to do some serious fishing. Gas up and be ready. I am flying into Homestead later today and will call you upon landing. You are sure you are cool with this, brother?" I had to ask. We, meaning Alex, Javi and myself, are used to taking risks, and I really did not want to put him in harm's way if I could avoid it.

"John, I am in. Whatever you need, I trust you to do your part, and I'll do mine."

"There will be four of us aboard, plus you."

"What the fuck? You think I have a party boat?" he said, laughing.

"See you later, Bro. Get ready for a little Caribbean adventure," I said, hanging up the phone.

I turned to Javi. "Is Mel ready?"

"She'll be at the airport ready to go," Javi replied.

Just as he said that, our captain opened the cockpit door and walked out. Sitting down across from us, he said, "Major, we have received instructions to pick up Miss Melissa at the airport in Mexico City and continue with the three of you to Homestead Air Force Base in Florida. You are aware? Does she know where to meet the plane?"

"Yes, we are, Captain. And, yes, she knows to go to the private plane terminal. Thank you."

"When we land, please stay on board so we don't have to deal with customs or immigration in Mexico."

"Not a problem. Although Javier here was hoping for a

chimichanga with carne," I said, joking, because I really didn't know what a chimichanga was. I just loved to say it slowly.

"Perhaps Miss Melissa could pick up a few of those for all of us," said the captain, seriously. "There is a very good Mexican restaurant on the second floor of the terminal, right above the American Airlines counter."

"Yeah? Shit, why not? Javi, call Mel and go for it."

CHAPTER TWENTY-FIVE

Chicago, Illinois

"Joey, ride with me in the car. I have to catch a flight to Miami," said Alex, as he met up with Joey by the elevators. "My flight is about three hours plus. By the time I land, I want everything you can find on Colonel Abimbola Cruz, head of the Cuban Intelligence Directorate or DGI. He seems to have a home in Varadero Beach, or at least a headquarters of some kind. I need the location."

"I heard you are getting Ms. Muller's computer from your home. What do you need from that?"

"It seems these people have hacked into Julia's system and more than likely ours. I am hoping you can find a way to reverse that and hack back, or whatever you call it."

"I understand. Yes, there is probably a way I can do that. Is there something I should know, Mr. C.?"

"Joey, this is on a need-to-know basis. Do not repeat it to anyone else," Alex said and went on to give Joey the details of the abduction and why it was so important to get the information on the Cubans. "We are going to go to Varadero and bring Julia and Jackie back. I need exact locations, coordinates, satellite maps for our incursion by boat. You got it?"

"Yes, sir, I do. I'll get you in there and out."

"Now, what information do you have on Nikolas Akakios?" asked Alex, as the limo made its way to O'Hare Airport.

"His hedge fund has been very busy trading a number of stocks short – that is selling them while not owning them, hoping they drop in value. Then his hedge fund is going long or buying the stock with the hope they go up in value. This seems to be a trend they are setting up, somewhat different from their other standard trades. At the same time, from the nature of their trades, they are thinking the U.S. markets are headed down, while the European and Asian markets are headed up," Joey explained.

"How so?"

"They are selling short the S&P 500 Index and going long with the Nikkei and DAX indices via option trading."

"So they think the U.S. is going down while Europe and Asia are going up. I think I need Julia to make sense of that. Tell me, what stocks in particular are they trading? Is it something obvious?"

"Again, I've separated their normal tendencies from their new trading strategy," Joey began.

"When you say, new, what do you mean?"

"I've noticed that they have established what I am calling new trading strategies in the last two weeks or so," replied Joey, looking at his files.

"Got it. Go on."

"In any case, there are three sectors they are trading, the banking, retail stores, and electronic manufacturing sectors. Within those sectors, they are trading three stocks each, for a total of nine stocks."

"What do you make of that?"

"Mr. C., if the reason we are investigating them is to uncover corporate espionage and insider trading, then I would guess that they are laying the groundwork and establishing a pseudo stock trading strategy to disguise their ultimate goal. They could not just trade the one stock they may want. If challenged, they want to prove to the Securities and Exchange Commission that they have a trading strategy they are pursuing based on sector rotation or whatever the lingo is."

Alex opened his eyes wide as he looked at Joey. "We need to start playing the market when I come back, Joey."

Joey smiled with those big white teeth dominating his face from ear to ear.

"Concentrate on this Abimbola character now," said Alex, as the limo approached the gate. "Nothing else is more important than getting the info we need to infiltrate into Varadero. Is that clear?"

"Yes, Mr. C. I know you will be successful in getting both ladies out. As John likes to say, go for it."

Alex wasted no time. He literally jumped out of the limo and headed to the private plane terminal. A private

Gulfstream, owned by a client, was waiting for him. His mind was racing as he tried to play out all the variables involved in successfully getting Julia and Jackie out. He hoped Jackie was still alive. He wondered if it had been a mistake hiring Jackie after the takedown of Rick Ramirez in Miami and his phantom corporate success with MonteCarlo Industries. Jackie had had an opportunity to get lost and join the witness protection plan. He would have to deal with the outcome of this scenario at a later time. Right now, he needed to work out the logistics of this mission. He looked out the window as the Gulfstream swiftly took off and saw a beautiful blue sky above, the sun beginning its move to the west, and his adopted city of Chicago below. Would he ever see them again?

CHAPTER TWENTY-SIX

Shanghai, China

It was morning already halfway around the world. Director Cong Wáng, as he was known outside China, was up as usual at four in the morning. His evening companion, a non-consenting boy of twelve years old, was whisked away by servants, as was the customary procedure in the mornings. Director Chen Lee, his real name in China, had quite the day ahead of him. Actually, it might be a day and a night.

His cyber team staff was ready for today. They had planned and completed dry runs in the past few days. Today's cyber attacks would not be much different from the ones they had done in the past. However, today's attacks would be coordinated with their U.S. and world partners to profit from the trading in the stocks of the targeted companies.

Cyber attacks had become a constant occurrence everywhere in the world. For most, it was hard to fathom that a government could actually carry out attacks of this nature. Most people whose accounts or identity had been hacked thought of a cyber criminal sitting at an Internet café somewhere in Romania. And while that did occur with frequency, the leap from that to an organized attempt by a country's government was to many, unthinkable.

Disruption, chaos, arrogance, profits were but a few of the many motivations behind Chen Lee's attacks on companies worldwide, although there was a certain added pleasure for him in attacking U.S. companies.

The attack on Elo Teck was more than just a hack to disrupt or steal customer information. Elo Teck was a super prize for Lee. The firm's plans for new drones, designed for the U.S. Department of Defense, were of major interest to China's military hierarchy.

Arriving at the office at his usual time of six in the morning, Lee went about his usual activities. One added twist today was a meeting with two of his young cyber geeks who had been working on various electrical grids within the United States. They had hacked into these grids and had the capability of taking these systems down at will. The objective could be rolling blackouts in various parts of the country or selected areas. It was like a board game to them. With a map of the U.S. in front of them, his boys could affect an electrical blackout at will anywhere on the map. All Lee had to do was point at a region, state, city, or whatever.

Operation Black Swan was about to happen in the next few days, and Lee wanted to have a maximum disruption effect. He already knew that eighteen Islamic terrorists had made it safely into the U.S. Their objectives were varied.

Some were headed to the Northeast—New York City, of course. Wall Street and surrounding areas would be targets for the bombings. Others had headed to Chicago. Their target - the Chicago Mercantile Exchange. Others had been given softer targets, such as malls, movie complexes, and tourist locations like Pier 39 in San Francisco and Disneyland in Anaheim, California. He personally had planned and coordinated—perhaps choreographed was a better description—all of the activities associated with the operation.

Director Lee had just lit a cigarette when General Dang Wu walked unannounced into his small office. Lee sprung up and stood at attention.

"General, good morning. What can I do for you?"

"Good morning, Director. Have a seat, please."

Lee put out his cigarette and waited for the general to sit down before he sat down. "General, what may I get for you?"

"Director, I am interested in today's activities in your department. Give me a preview. Then I want a schedule of events for the day that we go with Operation Black Swan."

"Of course, General. My pleasure. Today at eight in the evening here and eight in the morning in the United States, we are breaching the security of a retailer called SuperStore and a bank called SunMarc. Both of these companies will be made aware of the breach and the confidential nature of the information that has been copied and retrieved. The New York Stock Exchange will receive notification of both of these cyber attacks, prompting it to hold off on opening trading on these stocks at nine-thirty in the morning as usual. Once the NYSE opens, information about the systems being hacked will be devastating to the value of their stock. We are in a position to benefit from this adverse reaction to the stock prices, as well as to the prices of similar stocks in these sectors that should suffer, albeit not to the same degree, with the decline," explained the director, with a certain pride in his voice and poise in his posture.

"Very good, Director. What about the electronics manufacturer?" the general asked.

"General, we will be finalizing the breach and gathering all the plans for the design and manufacture of the drones by Elo Teck. However, we are not going to make them aware of the hack until they themselves find out. We are, however, in a position to profit from a decline in their stock and in the stock of two other similar manufacturers, once they make public the fact they were hacked."

"Will they, or perhaps I should ask, must they?"

"If they were a private company, I assume they would not release any information. However, the fact they are a public company will force them to release the fact of the breach of their security. I suspect they may want to delay to see if anyone claims to have hacked them. Or to see if they can trace the hack. Should they delay too long, we have ways to release the information anonymously and accomplish our objective with the stock trades. No matter what, we will have the plans for both drones, General," said Lee, smiling and looking directly into the general's eyes.

"Fantastic, Director Lee. Fantastic."

"Thank you, General."

"Now, tell me about the sequence of events being unleashed on America the day we go live with your baby, Operation Black Swan." Director Lee flashed a smile. Hearing the general calling it his baby made him very proud, and he knew he would, in fact, be recognized amongst his peers for his success in bringing the United States to its knees.

"General, let me give you the big picture. Then I will delineate in detail the particulars. We have the terrorist attacks set to go in the morning right after the stock market opens. The New York Stock Exchange opens at nine-thirty in the morning. They may delay the opening if we attack prior to that. Our computers are ready to simulate the trades in the dark pools that will cause a panic in the markets once they are spotted. Our calculations are the Dow Jones index will drop approximately seven to ten percent in a matter of minutes. At that point, the market may shut down as the officials try to come up with an explanation or excuse, and, or just shut down due to the safety triggers being exercised. Of course, our partners in New York have positioned our interests in such a way that we will benefit greatly from this drop and from the fear about the safety of trading stocks in the U.S. markets. Once they open the markets again, I am prepared to shut down the electrical grid in the Northeast of the United States. This will signal, for sure, that there is some form of organized terrorist attack under way," Lee said.

"Director, is this what you called the black swan effect?" asked the general.

Smiling from ear to ear, Director Lee replied, "Indeed, General, indeed."

"Director, I am satisfied with this big picture. Thank you so very much."

CHAPTER TWENTY-SEVEN

Homestead, Florida

Our flight from Mexico City to Homestead Air Force Base was incredibly smooth and comfortable, to say the least. Flying commercial after these two flights, well, it was something I didn't think I could do. Mel was panic-stricken after blaming herself, unjustly, for allowing Julia and Jackie to be kidnapped. I tried to console her by pointing out that what she did by escaping and getting the information she retrieved was more than anyone would expect. She was a fighter, and to her any kind of setback was a failure. After a while, she was able to calm down and put things in perspective, realizing there was really nothing she could have done to prevent what had happened.

Javi made her feel better by distracting her with various off-subject conversations. I could see that there was a little attraction between Javi and Mel. I didn't know where that would lead, but on that front I would let nature take its course.

As we landed at the air force base, we bid good-bye to the crew of the Gulfstream. After all these hours together we had begun a bit of bonding. I would have enjoyed continuing this bonding a little longer with our agent or fight attendant, Christine. It had been a pleasure to watch her move about the cabin. I know I sound like the typical male chauvinist. However, if you could see this young lady with jet-black long hair—I mean long in the back, all the way to the entrance to the valley – and with deep emerald green eyes accentuated by perfect black eyebrows that mesmerized you simply by looking at them. She was wearing a white blouse, maybe a size too small, over a frontal exposure that could weaken the knees of a king. Well, if you could see all this, I guess you would understand. I was in lust... no, I mean in love with this beautiful lady. So, I waved good-bye and felt a slight drop.

Back to business. Alex made his entrance by helicopter a few minutes after we landed. His flight had taken him to the Miami airport, and from there he had taken a short copter ride to us. His private plane ride, being a corporate-owned plane, had not been cleared to land at the base.

Alex made his way to Mel. They embraced and both cried quietly for a moment. It immediately brought back the reason why we were there. Good Lord! Julia and Jackie kidnapped by cartel gang members and then flown to Cuba as hostages or bait to get Alex. What a turn of events- from chasing terrorists in the tunnels between Mexico and the U.S. to planning a covert entry into Cuba to rescue family held as hostages. Javi and I had done this as Delta Force members but never to retrieve family. Alex, too, as a CIA operative had been involved in operations similar to this, but again, never when family was involved. Alex and Julia had gone from planning a wedding to this incredible situation. My heart felt for them. Failure, to use an old cliché, was not an option.

"John, is your brother ready?" Alex asked. After a few minutes of commiseration, he was back to all business.

"He is, Boss. He thinks we can make to Varadero in less than five hours."

"Let's plan our approach on the way to Islamorada. I have Joey calling me in a few minutes, hopefully with details of this character, Abimbola, who is holding both ladies. I think our driving time is about an hour. Is the car ready?"

"Yes, Mr. C. We have a black GMC SUV, ready and loaded with the equipment you requested," replied Javi from a few feet away as he opened the driver's door to the SUV.

"Let's go for it," I said as we boarded. Javi was driving, me in the passenger side, and Alex and Mel in the back. The equipment Alex had requested was enough to invade a small country. I was hoping we would not have to use it all. Big Brother James was going to shit in his shorts once he saw what we were bringing on board his pristine boat.

It took us exactly an hour to arrive at Marker 81.5 on the Overseas Highway. Eighty-one more miles and we would be all the way to the end of Key West where there is an ocean side sign saying ninety miles to Cuba.

Captain James's boat, a thirty-four-foot Pursuit 34 Express with twin inboard Volvo diesel engines, was docked at the World Wide Sportsman's Bayside Marina. Fortunately, this boat had a cabin, a head, and air conditioning. The "catchalottafish" was gassed and ready for its first expedition not related to catching a lot of fish.

"Permission to come on board, Captain?" I said to my brother James as we approached his spot in the marina. He turned around and looked up with a broad smile. He was hosing down the boat, a reflection of his anal personality when it came to his pride and beauty. He didn't get out much.

"Welcome aboard, little Johnny and guests. How the hell are you, Bro?" he said, as we embraced strongly, followed by mutual pats on the back.

"Doing great, man, doing great," I replied. "Let me introduce you to the members of your charter." So I did. I introduced him to Mel, as he helped her on board, then Javi, and finally, Alex.

"Captain, we have a few items to bring on board. Is there any kind of cart with wheels we can use?" asked Javi, looking around.

"You can find a couple of large carts with wheels right in the bait shop. Let me help you," Captain James replied, as he and Javi walked in the direction of the bait shop.

"Hang in there, guys," Javi said to the three of us. "The captain and I will get our supplies."

Javi and Big Brother made two trips back and forth between the SUV and the boat. Fortunately, our equipment consisting of weapons of various kinds and an assortment of firepower and ammunition was all inside metal and plastic boxes. Otherwise, the locals might have called a SWAT team to deal with us. People were very curious about what the hell we were bringing on board. But being the Keys, they were all chill and went about their own business. While at the base, we had acquired MREs or military rations, the best way to bring food for a couple of days of travel, and Captain James had secured drinking water and our favorite way to quench a thirst... beer. However, we would save the beer along with a few Padrón cigars I had brought with me for the return celebratory trip. I knew Alex did not like buying Cuban cigars as long as the Castro murderers were still in control of his homeland and would benefit from any cigar purchase. Not that the four or five dollar profit to the Communist regime would make any difference. With Alex, it was the principle of the matter. I understood and respected that so my Padrons were from Nicaragua, where the Padrón family had been making their cigars since 1964. My personal favorite was the Dámaso, named after the 19th century founder of Padrón Cigars in Cuba. It had a milder taste that I enjoyed, so "make mine a number four, please."

I knew Alex was partial to the Family Reserve cigar with a Maduro wrapper. So naturally I had a few of those. But the beers and cigars would have to wait.

"Captain, what is the course you are setting?" I asked my brother. We had completed loading the boat, the engines were on, and we were casting out lines on the dock.

The sun was just about to set. Tourists flock like hypnotized zombies every evening in the Keys to see the sunset. It did not matter how many days you stayed there on your visit or how many times you would go back. At sunset, you walked towards the bayside, then faced west, and watched the sunset. And, of course, you took pictures. This ritual happened to match the end of happy hour that might have something to do with the zombie-like behavior of those watching. In any case, I would not mind seeing a few of those sunsets. Tonight it was clear of clouds. The sky and the bay were silvery in color, like a mirror; they were almost indistinguishable from each other. Only the bright orange setting sun gave you the perspective of the sky meeting the waters of the bay, as the sun made its golden road east towards us, inviting us to follow it. It was mesmerizing to see all the colors as the Master of all artists with strokes, slowly and perfectly placed one after another, brushed them on the canvas of the sky.

My brother replied, breaking the spell the sunset had cast over me. "John, the GPS route from my dock to

Varadero Beach Cuba is 163.57 statute miles, or 142.14 nautical miles. The coordinates for Varadero Beach, Cuba, are 23°09´24″N, 81°14´39″ W. It should take us, if the weather holds, about four and one-half hours to reach there. Do we know where to make land, or maybe I should say, where not to make land?"

"Captain, I am waiting for communication about that. I should know exactly in a while. Is that an issue now?" asked Alex, still waiting for Joey to give us some kind of heads-up from his research."

"No, not at all, sir. We still have quite some time to go. Plus Varadero is very small anyway. We can make corrections anytime," replied Captain James.

"Great, Captain. Please call me Alex. As soon as I get a call, I'll inform you of any information that may change our coordinates."

We all sat back as we made our way to Cuba. Everyone was wearing a life vest. The Pursuit was symmetrically cutting the ocean, pushing out that white foam from the sides of the boat. Night was approaching, and I could not help to see how cozy Javi and Mel had made themselves, sitting side by side, covered by a blanket. Huh! As the evening got cooler, they both moved down from the back of the boat and into the cabin. Less windy, I guess.

CHAPTER TWENTY-EIGHT

Straits of Florida

The roar of the engines became one with the night and we seemed to be floating our way over the ocean. Suddenly the sound of the sat phone broke the stillness. It was Joey. Alex picked up and spoke to him for about five minutes, repeating things a couple of times to remember them.

Alex motioned me to come inside the cabin and we all sat around the table next to the galley. "Captain, let's bring the boat to idle for a moment so I can review a few things," he said. Javi and Mel joined the rest of us. "OK, here is the scoop. We have our landing spot and our plan for retrieval of Julia and Jackie. Joey found the exact address of Colonel Abimbola's compound. Not only that, he has been able to hack into ..." A huge bolt of lightning hit in front of our boat followed by a walloping thunderous clash. It seemed that if we had not come to idle the bolt would have landed right on the boat. We all looked at each other with consternation. Captain James's weather radar showed a storm with all the orange and red colors moving our way, from east to west. Squalls broke out, with the winds picking up gusts to forty miles per hour, and the seas erupted from calm to about eight-foot-high waves in a matter of minutes. The boat began to rock as we headed into a front.

"How are we doing, Captain?" I asked my brother, as I made my way out of the cabin and up to the helm.

"Brother, we are in a middle of a nasty storm. Hope you guys can stomach this. Otherwise, the head is right there for you. From the looks of it, it might take us a few minutes to get out of it. Maybe twenty to thirty," said Captain James.

"Roger that, Bro. I'll pass the word on," I said, walking down to the galley again and repeating what the captain had said to everyone sitting around the table. Mel gave me a shitty look and stuck her fingers in her mouth, as if to tell me she might be throwing up anytime now. As I walked over, I knocked on the door to the head and motioned to her to let her know where to go if need be. She nodded and smiled. It took us exactly thirty minutes to get out from under the storm, just as my big brother had estimated. But it seemed like an hour, bouncing from side to side with heavy rains, wind, lightning, and thunder. As we pulled out, we could see the storm front moving west, taking with it all the nastiness. James asked me to take the helm for a few minutes, and he sat back and relaxed a bit from the stress of steering the boat through that mess.

"Do we have a location for landing yet?" he asked, with his eyes closed and his head back.

"I am sure Alex will bring you up to date any moment.

How long before we get close to the Cuban coast?" I inquired.

"Not very long. We need to be aware of their coast guard ships real soon. I say maybe an hour now that the seas are so flat."

I followed the GPS route that my brother had programmed into the navigation system. The radar screen was clear, no storm, no other boats or bleeps on it. About twenty minutes later, he asked me if I wanted him to take over. Alex had briefed Captain James below. They had agreed to come into Varadero from the Bay of Cardenas. Varadero was part of a peninsula called Hicacos. It stuck out in a northeasterly fashion from the mainland. The north side facing the Florida Straits is about twelve miles of incredibly pure white sandy beach with crystal clear blue and emerald green waters. The bay side had its shallow areas but also had some beach coves. It was mostly mangroves. Our entrance would be better from this side as opposed to the exposed beachfront. Suddenly I heard and saw a bleep on the radar. I turned to James. "Bro, we have company," I said with some concern.

"Let me take over," he said, moving in behind the wheel and looking at the radar.

"It looks like a boat is moving in a direction that will cross with us in about twenty minutes. It could be a Cuban fishing boat, or it could be one of their coast guard ships," he said looking at me.

Sticking my head back in the cabin, I said, “We may have company in a few minutes. We need to evade this boat that is soon to be near us.”

Alex’s eyes opened wide. “Javi, get the red plastic box we brought on board.”

“The long one, Boss?” Javi asked.

“Yes, the long one. I was going to unveil this baby in Varadero. But we might as well break it open now,” Alex said.

“What is it, Boss?” I asked.

“It’s a prototype from one of our clients, Elo Teck,” he said as he undid the side fasteners and began opening the container.

“What kind of prototype, Boss?” asked Javi.

“It’s a surveillance drone, equipped with cameras that can relay a live feed right into this monitor,” Alex replied, pointing to the small monitor he was holding in his hand.

“Boss, it looks similar to what we have used for the agency the past couple of years,” I said.

“It is, John. But look at the size of this one,” he said. “Have you ever seen anything this small?”

“Shit, no, can’t say that I have,” I said. “Can you fly that, Boss?”

“I can, and so can Mel,” Alex replied.

“Get out. She can?”

"Indeed, she can. Jackie taught her how and she's damn good at it," he replied.

Mel was standing there, smiling from ear to ear. "What kind of training you think I've had, John?" Mel asked.

"Had no idea you learned how to fly a drone that small." I said.

"Size does not matter," Mel said.

"Say that again," Javi chimed in.

"Let me be specific. No, not on a drone. I am flying it while looking at a screen. I don't care how big or small the actual drone is," she said.

"Guys, the other boat is getting near. I am going to maneuver away. But if you have plans to deploy that machine, better do it now," Captain James said.

"Get it up in the air, Mel. Fly it to the boat, and let's see who is coming. Then we can deal with it. And, it is not a machine, Captain. It's an unmanned aerial vehicle or UAV," replied Alex.

Captain James turned to me and said, "John, can you imagine what I can do with that little UAV to spot dolphins and tuna? Man, it would be like cheating. Go out to a depth of eight hundred to one thousand feet, deploy the bird, and search comfortably without gunning and running. I love it! Mr. C., I think I found a way for you to repay me."

"Let's get through this operation, and we'll see, Captain," responded Alex.

Mel had the bird in the air now, flying towards the other ship. No need to fly too high since it was very dark out there, and the crew in the other ship were not going to see it. This was coming in handy here and I could see why Alex brought it. We were outnumbered in Cuba, and this little bird was going to prove very handy when we got there.

"Captain James," Alex began, "if it's the Cuban coast guard, can we outrun it?"

"Doubtful. Even if we did, we are going into Cuba. They'll have more coming out at us from the sea and the air, don't you think?" Captain James asked.

"Yeah, you are right," Alex said.

I was sitting there wondering what the hell was going to happen if this, in fact, was the Cuban coast guard. We had the fighting power, I knew, 'cause Alex had brought some heavy armament on board. But was that the way out of this? I stood behind Mel looking at the monitor to see if I could see anything. Finally, lights below. From the perspective of the drone, the camera was aiming down, and we could see lights. Mel flew it down closer, and when the image came into focus, we could see it was not the coast guard or a gunboat of any kind. In fact, it was a fishing boat going out to sea. All we had to do was get out of its way and we were golden.

"Boss," Mel began, "it's a fishing boat, boys. No guns, no military."

"Sounds good to me," Captain James said. "I'll get out of its way. Hang on."

With that, James brought the boat back on a plane, going west first and then making a turn to the southeast. Mel, in turn, flew that little bird back on board. The fishing boat went by north of us without any consequence whatsoever. We continued tracking the coordinates that had been set for Varadero. We were out about thirty to forty minutes from reaching our destination. Still, with the cover of night, we should be making land around one in the morning. Our plan was to retrieve Julia and Jackie and be out of there with plenty of time to leave under the cover of night. The darkness was our friend. Alex was not expected for another two days, and although Colonel Abimbola's compound would be well guarded, our belief was that they would not be expecting us there tonight. So we made our final plans for disembarking. Captain Big Brother James would stay with the boat and pretend to be preparing for a charter out of Varadero Marina should anyone ask. Alex and Javi would make their way to just outside the colonel's home or compound and wait for my intelligence report. Mel would be with me. She was my spotter as I was back in my old role as a sniper. Also, she would be flying the little bird above and around the home giving the three of us the lay of the land. As soon as Alex and Javi made it in, I would join them once the outside guards had been neutralized. Mel would continue to do reconnaissance in and around the home. As we stepped out of the home with J. and J., she would direct us to Captain James along the best possible route.

"I see lights ahead. We are approaching Varadero," said Captain James.

"How are you going to do this?" asked Alex.

"I am going to come in through the Bay of Cardenas side as discussed. So I have to go to the northernmost point of the peninsula and then make a turn south and west. There are some shallow areas we need to look out for according to my charts. Once we make the turn, I'll drop you off a few blocks from this guy's compound," replied Captain James.

As we were waiting for my big bro to find our spot, Mel asked Alex, "Mr. C., have you been here before?"

In a low voice and with some sadness, Alex replied, "As a child, Mel. I remember my dad would bring us here for the summer vacation. We would rent a home and spend almost three months here. I have some fond memories of the beach and the park where we roller-skated and biked. Varadero Beach became a tourist resort for the elite around the 1870s. Known for its white sandy beaches and its blue-green crystal clear waters, it attracted the well to do in its early days. An American millionaire, Mr. Irénée du Pont, built a mansion in the 1930s on the northernmost point of the island and really was responsible for the influx of tourists after that. The rich and famous and also the infamous, such as Al Capone, made Varadero a regular vacation spot. Today the airport is the second most important airport in Cuba, after the airport in Havana."

We were idling now, slow and easy, as we made our way to a set of docks that seemed abandoned. It was after one in the morning, so we did not expect too many people on this side of Varadero.

"Javi, please get the bow line. I am going to put it in on the port side. John, you handle the stern line, please. As soon as Javi is on the dock, I am turning the engines off," said Captain James in a low voice, almost whispering.

"Does everyone know their assignments?" asked Alex, whispering.

We all replied in the affirmative. The lives of Julia and Jackie were on the line. Of course, if we were caught, it was all over for us, too. There was no one prepared to extract us from this location. No helicopters waiting for a signal. No marines to come ashore. We were on our own in a non-sanctioned operation only a handful of people knew about. The SEALs, the other guys, had a slogan, "the only easy day was yesterday." Boy, was that the case here today. I had my own, and I said softly, "Let's go for it," as we began to disembark from my brother's boat.

CHAPTER TWENTY-NINE

Varadero Beach, Cuba

Let the fear of danger be a spur to prevent it; he that fears not, gives advantage to the danger.

– Francis Quarles

Mel and I made our way first. Our job was to be on overwatch for Alex and Javi as they made their way to the compound. We had no idea of what to expect or what kind of force was waiting for us. General Patton would have kicked our asses had we presented this attack plan to him for evaluation. The general was famous for his reconnaissance flights across enemy lines, which he flew with a pilot. His success was partly due to his preparation. Knowing where the enemy was and how they were positioned was a key factor in launching a successful attack. I was thinking about what the general could have done with these drones we had today? In our case, we had jack shit. It was makeshift, by the seat of our pants, like. So, Mike Tyson's saying, "Everyone has a plan, "till they get punched in the mouth," was our strategy today. I made the calculation that we had been punched in the mouth and now the plan was fluid. We crossed Autopista Sur, a road that went the length of the peninsula on the bayside. Our next objective was crossing Avenida 1ra, or First Avenue, and then reaching Avenida Playa where the homes facing the beach, including Abimbola's compound, would be.

"Mel, hang on, there is a car coming," I said, as we reached an intersection.

"Put your hand over my shoulder. Quick," she said.

I did. And she came in close to me and put her hand behind my back. We both dropped our packs full of goodies, as we stood there pretending to be a couple out for a walk.

"What if they stop us?" she asked.

"If they stop us, first, we are Canadian tourists. Alex got passports for all of us with Canadian identities."

"What names?"

"Our own. We had no time to learn a new identity. Just go with the flow."

"Very well. You said, first, we are Canadians. What is second, eh?"

"Quick learner. Did you ever read any of Vince Flynn's books with Mitch Rapp, an ex-CIA operative, as his main character?"

"No, I can't say that I have. Why?"

"Well, if our Canadian tourist story does not work, then we become American assassins. Which happens to be the title of one of his books. *¿Comprende?*"

"Roger that."

A fairly new car drove by with the occupants looking at us. It looked like two men in the front seat. New cars were not a common scene in Cuba. Only government personnel would be driving one. Cuba had stood still since 1959, the last year before the Communist regime took over. What was common was to see forty-year-old cars everywhere. The ingenuity of these people to keep those antiques running was incredible. I turned against Mel, facing the direction of the car so I could follow it with my eyes.

"What you doing, big boy, eh?"

"Just hang on. I am looking at the car to see if it makes any sudden turns."

"Any excuse to ... Wow! I hope that's your Glock I am feeling."

This young lady was a character. I laughed. "As a matter of fact, it is my Glock."

She smiled and quipped back, "You have a silencer on it already, eh?

"The car's gone. Let's move on and find a spot to set up. Alex and Javi should not be too far behind."

"Guys, remember we are all connected with COM systems," Alex's voice came into our ears.

"We are good, Boss, very few people around. I think I found my overwatch spot. Let you know as soon as we are set up and we launch our little bird," I replied.

"Why are you feeling his Glock," Javi asked.

"Alex, did you know they call Javi *La Puta*?" I remarked, trying to change the conversation. I had an idea why Javi was not happy about my Glock.

"I don't want to hear a word unless it has to do with our operation. Got it?" Alex commanded in a stern voice. "One click for 'yes,' two for 'no.' Otherwise, shut the hell up."

I clicked mine three times. "Javi, stop that shit," I said. I could imagine Alex, really pissed, looking at Javi and Javi looking back, shaking his head at him.

Most of the private homes along the beach were owned by the regime, as was everything else on this Communist island. It was in the 1960s when these homes had been confiscated by Castro and his band of thieves. Colonel Abimbola's home or compound was no exception. I found an empty two-story home diagonally across from our target's home. It was perfect and looked as if it were built in the '40s. What was perfect was the roof, a flat roof with a parapet around it. The parapet was a three-foot wall that surrounded the roof and would serve my needs exactly. Mel followed me as we broke in quietly and made our way to the second story and the roof. "Mel, remind me to tell you later what realtors mean by a two-story home."

"John, are you in place yet?" asked Alex, still pissed.

"Three more minutes, Boss." As soon as we reached the rooftop, we took out the little bird and Mel sat with her back against the ledge prepared to propel it into the air. "We are ready to launch."

"We are two blocks away from your location. Wait. I can't believe it," said Alex, sounding amazed.

"What is it, Boss?" I asked.

"Mel, get the bird up. There's a jeep fumigating for mosquitoes. Can you see it?" Alex asked.

I replied, "I see a vehicle with a lot of smoke being pushed out of one side. Is that what you are referring to?"

"Exactly. Mel, if you fly the drone above the jeep, the noise of the fumigating will drown out any sound the drone makes. That jeep goes back and forth on every street," Alex replied.

"Why did you say you could not believe it?" asked Mel.

"Because when I was a kid, and we vacationed here, all the kids would follow the jeep on our bicycles. It was a blast and cool with all the white smoke being pumped out. You could not see us as we would be enveloped by the smoke."

"Kids did that at two in the morning?" I asked.

"That jeep came around two or three times in the evening. Who knows what we were inhaling back then?" Alex said.

"Well, at least we know you are not a mosquito. Besides, I bet your parents smoked in the car with the windows closed and you wore no seatbelts."

"Roger that. Let it fly, Mel. We are right below you and ready to proceed. We have serious work to do here," Alex said.

Mel began flying the bird in an ascending fashion, following the fumigating vehicle. It was going to take her to the house and around it. She was going to get a perfect view of any sentries who might be located on the roof of the compound. I, in turn, put on my night vision goggles and concentrated on the roof across from me. Colonel Abimbola's compound took up an entire square block. When they confiscated these homes they must have created this compound that consisted of four houses. Now, an eight-foot wall surrounded the property with two entrances, one on the north side and the other on the west side. From my vantage point, I could tell the north entrance was the main entry, and the west was for military and service personnel. Most of the lights in the home were off.

"Mel, do you see anything yet?" I asked.

"I see three sentries on their flat roof. Two are together and they seem to be smoking. They are on the south side of the roof. The other is standing above the north entrance and seems to be talking to someone below him," she replied.

"Copy that. I see the idiots smoking. That's a no-no. But I guess they don't expect anything. That cigarette can be seen a long ways away if someone is looking for them. I also see the one guy on the north side. And there is, in fact, at least one more sentry on the main entrance," I said for everyone to hear.

The sound of the vehicle going around as it fumigated

was excellent cover for the drone, now flying directly on top of the compound.

"Alex, I only see the one sentry on the north entrance on the grounds. Let me make another full sweep of the grounds to be sure," said Mel.

"While she does that, let me say, Alex, I can take out the three guys on the roof in fairly quick succession. I'll tap the two together and move immediately to the guy on the north side. But I cannot have him talking to the guy on the ground while I do that, for obvious reasons."

"Roger that, John," Alex said. "Wait for Mel to complete her second sweep and be ready to go one, two, three. When you do, Javi and I will enter from the south side. We'll be climbing the walls rather easily—and quickly, of course. We'll move north to neutralize the ground sentry. Mel, be sure to keep that bird over the compound. You are our only eyes."

"You bet, Boss. No worries there," Mel replied. "No one else on the grounds at this point. The lone sentry on the roof over the north side gate is no longer talking to anyone on the ground. As a matter of fact, this guy is taking a piss. And I didn't have to zoom to see that. Wow! That guy is definitely Cuban."

"You've been hanging around Jackie too long. Boss, on the count of five, I am taking these guys out. One, two, three, four, five."

I fired my M24 Remington, which was equipped with a night vision scope. Pop, pop. Turn to the north. Pop. Three shots to the head. Three men down."

"This is Mel. Three confirmed down on roof. No movement. They are down for good."

"Roger that. We are going over the wall," Alex said. "Mel, keep that bird up there. John, make your way to the north entrance."

"Ahead of you, Boss," I said, as I had already left the house without waiting for confirmations on my hits.

I could hear Alex and Javi over the COM system, as they were moving slowly in the direction of the north entrance to take out the fourth guy. I heard three suppressed pops in my ear and waited for any word.

"John, we are opening the north gate."

"Already there."

As I entered the compound, I saw Javi with his right knee on the chest of the guard and his Glock inside the guy's mouth. "What's going on?" I asked. "You didn't kill him?"

"Not yet. I need information," Alex replied.

"What about the shots I heard?"

"One in each shoulder so he would drop his gun, the third on a knee so he would go down easily," said Alex, looking a bit proud of himself.

"Good shooting, Javi," I said, looking at Javi.

"Fuck you, John boy," replied Alex. "Javi, has he said

anything?"

"I'll ask him again. This time I'll take my Glock out of his mouth," said Javi. *"Si no quieres que te pegue un tiro en la cabeza, dime donde están las dos mujeres."*

I understood shot, head, and women. So I got the picture. This guy was already hurting from the three shots. Not only that, there was also a considerable amount of blood pooling around him. I saw Alex walk over and step on the guy's shoulder. The man gasped, and as he opened his mouth to scream, Alex inserted his suppressed Glock into the guy's mouth once again. The guy's eyes almost popped out. *"Mira, no tengo tiempo para perder, si quieres morir en este instante, no hables. Si quieres vivir, contesta la pregunta. Mueve la cabeza si vas a contestar,"* Alex said, removing his foot from the man's shoulder.

This time I understood time, death, live, and head. I had no fucking clue what was just said. But the man understood quite well because I saw Alex removing his Glock from the man's mouth and kneeling down to listen to him. They spoke some more. Alex nodded to Javi, and Javi inserted a needle into the guy's arm.

"Propofol?" I asked.

"He'll sleep while we go to work," Javi replied.

"OK, Julia and Jackie are in the second house. The fucking colonel is in this house, in the front. John and I are going to walk around the side of this house and enter the second house. Javi, I want you here to protect our flank and exit point. Three quick clicks on the COM system if someone comes out of the main house or you see anything else," Alex said. "Mel, anything to report?"

"All quiet, no movements."

"Captain James, all good by you?"

We got one click back from Big Bro. Translation: all good.

"Very well, let's go for it," Alex said.

"I like that, Boss," I said, smiling at Alex for picking my slogan. We moved cautiously and quietly around the side of the main home housing Abimbola. The second house was two stories, a beautiful wood-framed home, same as Abimbola's. The ladies we now knew were upstairs. We expected two guards only on the lower floor, both of whom should be sleeping as we had learned from our talkative friend by the north gate.

The front door was unlocked. The house was dark. Both Alex and I put on our night vision goggles and moved swiftly through the house, him going right and me left. As I entered a room, I heard two pops. I assumed it was Alex. I popped my guy twice as he awoke from what little sound Alex had made. I said, "Clear."

Alex replied through his COM, "Clear. Headed upstairs."

"Right behind you."

We walked slowly and quietly again up the stairs. Like felines staying close to the walls, we made our way up. Finally we reached the landing. There was one room to the right and one room to the left. Alex signaled with his head for me to go right, as he made a turn to the left. I made my way into a room.

CHAPTER THIRTY

New York City

Nikolas Akakios had not been able to sleep a wink. His condominium in Central Park West where he spent the weekdays was luxurious and lavish. He was anxious and to add to his frustration, he was horny. He and Marta Oliva, who played many roles in his life, were not sexually active. Their intimacy had terminated early in their relationship, particularly soon after she involved him in her religion. Sex with her, twenty years his junior, had been extremely rewarding for him, and he had always hoped they would resume those activities. But she had reached her goal in his household and in his business... total control of the man via her religion and his lust for her. He dated and had sexual encounters, but Marta preapproved them. Akakios trusted her beyond anything imaginable, and he allowed himself to be managed by her in many ways. Marta had the power to mcct and interview almost any new associate Akakios might consider...both personal as well as in business. Under the guise of consulting her "saints," she would have the last word.

This morning his anxiety was due to the events about to happen. It was related to Director Chen Lee and the manipulation of the three companies listed on the New York

Stock Exchange. Today's trades were not too different from other trades he had executed through his hedge fund and black pools earlier for the Chinese government. However, the stakes had gotten bigger as he, his associates, and the Chinese government moved closer to the culmination of Operation Black Swan. He knew the start of the operation would begin with these trades, followed by the events that the stock market would later call 'black swan events,' a series of unexpected events that would create chaos in the financial markets. Of course, for a few, these would not be unexpected events. In fact, these events were carefully planned and would be meticulously executed to deliver the second and third punch into an economy that was still recovering from the aftermath of September 11, 2001. The Standard and Poor's Index, a measure of the largest five hundred stocks in the United States, had been down 13 percent in the aftermath of 2001, after being down 10 percent in 2000. Two down years in the market had not been recorded since the 1970s when unemployment had exceeded 10 percent and interest rates had gone through the roof. Now in 2002, a third down year coupled with the weak economy could literally throw the U.S. into a recession or worse, a depression.

The goals of this unholy cabal were within reach. Akakios could feel it and wanted to do his share to bring about the new world order they planned.

Today would be Day One. Three United States companies would be hacked, exposing sensitive and private information not only on the company's inner workings, but also, more importantly, the private information of thousands of Americans, maybe hundred of thousands of Americans. Day Two would be the operation itself... a cyber-created flash crash of the stock market, directed by Director Lee's cyber group in Shanghai, starting at or about ten in the morning. This would be followed by multiple terrorist attacks on vulnerable soft targets in various parts of the country, all coordinated and well orchestrated. In the early afternoon, the cyber flash crash would be reversed, assuming the markets had remained open, and an unprecedented recovery would be manufactured. In the late afternoon, there would be a cyber attack on the electrical grids in the northeast and western states.

No wonder Akakios could not sleep and was awake at two in the morning. The next two days were to be the start of the fall of the United States. As he thought about that he began to feel exalted and aroused. He remembered a similar feeling when as a young twenty-year-old he had been taking flying lessons and found himself on his first solo flight one day. He was aroused, he noticed, as he was alone and felt exhilarated.

Akakios walked into Marta's room; he was not going to take "no" for an answer. As he walked in, Marta raised the sheets, exposing her entire naked body in the light of the moon rays as they shown in through the windows by her bed. Moving over to one side, she motioned and encouraged Akakios to join her in bed. Disrobing, Akakios felt his face flush, and with a full erection, he cuddled up to Marta's back.

Director Lee would be calling at six in the morning; Akakios had three hours to mollify his hunger and longing for her.

CHAPTER THIRTY-ONE

Varadero Beach, Cuba

I walked slowly into the room, not knowing what to expect. What I saw horrified me. Jackie, naked and chained to her bed, her face swollen from repeated beatings, her eyes almost shut involuntarily. Rage overtook me. My moniker, "The Hulk," was manifesting itself. I wanted to get Jackie and Julia out of there and blow this fucking compound to kingdom come. But first, I wanted this Colonel Abimbola. As I began unshackling Jackie, I could only imagine how Alex had found Julia. I prayed that she was not anywhere near how Jackie looked.

"Jackie, don't speak. Work with me a little. I am going to get you out of here. Can you walk?"

She mumbled something. I repeated myself. "Can you walk?"

"I don't know," she replied.

"Let's try. I need you to try, please, Jackie."

We began walking out of there. First, with a lot of effort, then she was able to stand erect and pick up the pace. As we did, I saw Alex coming with Julia from the other room. Thank God, Julia looked fine. She was alert and seemed unhurt. They both looked at Jackie.

"Oh, my God," Julia said softly.

"I am going to kill that son of a bitch," Alex exclaimed.

"You are going to have to wait in line," I said. "Let's get these ladies out of here.

Javi, we are coming out. We have Julia and Jackie."

"Roger that. We are clear from my end," Javi said through the COM system.

"You are clear from the bird's view," said Mel.

"Mel, get ready to help Julia and Jackie back to the boat. Javi, Alex and I will follow." I said into the COM system. Bro, are you listening? We have three ladies coming your way."

"Roger that. We are clear on my end. Same spot," Captain James said.

We walked down the stairs and out the door of this home. We moved cautiously towards Javi who had taken a position behind some bushes with a clear shot of the front door of Abimbola's home. Alex, still with Julia, moved ahead out of the front gate of the home and to a side of the eight-foot wall. Mel joined him there. With Javi on my rear, I helped Jackie walk, and we made it to the same spot. Mel gasped when she saw Jackie. I could only think that Mel was having flashbacks of her own torture at the hands of her stepfather and later in prison.

"Sorry. I had no makeup," Jackie said, trying to smile but in pain.

The ladies embraced each other.

"Mel, you know where to go. We have some business to

take care of here. We'll be right behind you," I said.

The three of them walked away in between the shadows and the darkness. "Let's go for it." Alex and I walked back into the compound. Javi had already begun to prepare the explosives- C-4 on timers. We set the timers for thirty minutes for the explosives around Abimbola's house. Thirty-five minutes for the ones we planted in the house that was used to hold Julia and Jackie. Our teamwork was to be commended. We worked as one, quiet and efficiently. As we left the compound and closed the door, we set additional explosives by the front gate to go off in forty minutes. We hoped this would give us enough time to make it around the Bay of Cardenas and into the Atlantic, heading north and east. The element of surprise was on our side, but they might figure out we came in by sea if anyone survived our explosives. These fucking guys were going to burn in these two wood homes. Like a matchbox.

The ladies were a few blocks ahead of us. The night was dark and the moon, while out and bright, was being covered by a wonderful set of low clouds that seemed to be part of our covert team.

Mel, Julia, and Jackie made it across Autopista Sur and into the mangrove area where Brother James had the boat docked.

"I see three ladies fifty yards away," Captain James said.

"Roger that," I replied. "We are right behind."

"Fuck, get down," Javi said, as a military jeep with four soldiers went right by us on their way to the compound.

"We need to hustle out of here, guys," I said, looking at my watch. "Ten more minutes before the first set of explosives goes off."

"Ladies on board," Captain James said.

"Great news, Brother. Get those twin Volvos ready; we'll be there in five."

I could hear Captain James telling Mel to undo the lines. He was going to punch it the second we stepped into the boat. I could not wait to feel that sea air blow right into my face and hear the rumbling of those engines. At the same time, I needed to hear our explosives go off and see that plume of smoke rise into the sky.

As we got ready to cross Autopista Sur, a military jeep with two soldiers came out of nowhere and stopped right in front of us.

"¿Como están, camaradas?" Alex asked the two soldiers.

"¿Que hacen aquí?" asked the driver.

"Tomando una copitas, hermano," replied Alex, saying we had been drinking.

"¿Que tienen en esas bolsas?" asked the driver in a demanding voice as he began to step out of the jeep.

The next few seconds happened in a blur. Alex used the

words we had always reserved for any emergencies. It was a command to take whatever action was required at the moment to get out of whatever predicament we might find ourselves in.

"Oklahoma," he said.

Javi went around the other side of the jeep as the soldier on the passenger side was stepping out. The guy never knew what hit him, as his neck was broken with two swift movements. At the same time, Alex dropped everything he was carrying and, as the soldier looked down, my right hand was already pushing him towards Alex whereupon his neck was snapped and broken. We put both soldiers back in the jeep, and Javi drove it onto a side road so it would not be seen for a while. All we needed was another five minutes before all hell broke loose. We double-timed it all one hundred yards that were left to board the Catchalottafish and get the hell out of Cuba.

Captain James had that Pursuit going at full speed as we were approaching the end point of the Varadero peninsula. Suddenly a dramatic explosion went off to the port side of the boat. That would be to our left. We could see the plume of black smoke rising into the sky. We smiled, not ready to celebrate yet. In the cabin, Julia told Jackie that the explosion was Abimbola's home. She smiled. A few minutes later another series of explosions went off, followed by a third. Our hope had been, if any survived the first and second, that the third might catch them as they ran out of the compound. Our next goal was going out twelve miles into the sea. This, we hoped, would keep any chasers at bay as territorial waters ended at twelve miles. That was, of course, assuming they would respect that – which we doubted if they had any inkling the attackers had been us.

CHAPTER THIRTY-TWO
Straits of Florida

Big Bro had those Volvo engines at full throttle. I could feel the reverberation all the way up my ass. My eyes were on the ocean, but my mind was with Jackie. I needed to get down in the cabin and be with her for a while. The last few days had been a horrifying experience for her. I knew she was in good hands in the company of Mel and Julia. But I just felt I had to be with her for a bit. Anyway, Alex, Javi, and I were looking in every direction as we cleared the northern tip of Varadero and headed north and east for Islamorada, Florida. The night was calm, and the moon, to our left or west of us, had covered itself while we pulled the operation on land. It seemed to know we could use some moonlight on the ocean to help get us out of Dodge. The seas had waves no more than one to two feet high, otherwise known as calm. Big Bro had some cool ones on ice. I don't know what it was, but drinking a beer would just put me in a Key West frame of mind. Also, he was ready to punch "play" on his sound system and let the King of the Conch Republic, Jimmy Buffet, blast us all the way home. However, all of that would have to wait. Alex got on the sat phone and spoke to someone.

"Bro, you think Alex can see his way to leave the drone

behind?" Captain James asked me.

"What drone, James?" I replied, looking perplexed.

"What do you mean 'what drone'? The drone, man! You know how my fishing business could improve if I had a drone I could deploy to look for dolphins and tuna."

"In the cabin, port side, in the storage compartment under the seat there is a box. If we forget it when we go back well... You follow, Brother?"

He looked at me, smiling from ear to ear. "How about some brews?" he asked.

"How far until we get to twelve miles out?"

"Five more miles," Captain James replied.

"Break out the music then. I'll serve *las frias* myself."

"*Las frias*? What's that?"

"The cold ones, the cold ones."

"Roger that."

"Boss, we are about five miles from the end of Cuban waters," I said to Alex, as he sat there quietly, probably rehashing what we had done and how close Julia and he had come to total devastation. I wasn't going to say it, but Julia was like a magnet for trouble. Noriega's goon in 1990 had wanted to kidnap her at best, and Alex was there to save her. Then in 2000, Cuban generals had wanted to assassinate all Cuban Council members and an attempt was made on her that killed her philandering husband and his mistress. And now, this character Abimbola actually succeeded in kidnapping her. Shit! What's up with that?

Alex did not reply. He looked at me and nodded, then headed down into the cabin to be with the ladies.

"So, why do they call Javi La Puta?" Captain James asked.

"That's right. I told you I would explain that one."

"It turns out we were in Puerto Rico one time on leave, back in the days of Special Forces. We were stationed at Fort Buchanan. Anyway, we were out one day, hotel casino hopping, and these beautiful women kept hitting on Javi. He was flabbergasted, and his chest was out like a fighting cock, he was so proud. He kept saying to us, 'man, these women are all over me, this is incredible.' So we said, go ahead man, break away from the pack, do your thing. Sure enough, the next lady we walked by hit on him. He waved us off and stayed behind with her. Five minutes later he was running to catch up with us. So we asked, 'what happened, brother?' 'No,' he said, 'not interested.' We kept on walking not thinking too much about it. Next hotel lobby, bang, another lady hit on him. We get waved off again. Instant replay, back with us in less than five minutes," I explained to James, with Javi looking not a bit too happy.

"What was going on?" Captain James asked with an incredulous look on his face.

"Bro, it turns out all these ladies were prostitutes. Putas, Brother! And he thought he was 'the man' before that."

"Why did they hit on him only?" Captain James wanted to know.

"He had been to a baptism in the morning at a church and was dressed in his Sunday best. So, they thought he had mula. We looked like our usual shitty selves and they had no interest in us. So, from that day forward, Javi became La Puta."

"You love telling that story, you son of a bitch," Javi said, smiling as he remembered that day.

"It looks like two people were baptized that day, the child and Javi," Captain James quipped.

"Never thought of that," I replied.

"Why don't you tell him part two of the story?" Javi said.

"Go ahead, you tell him," I said.

"Captain, at the end of the evening, I had met so many of these ladies that we got invited to their bar across from the hotels. Only pimps and call girls were there. So, we walked in and enjoyed ourselves until seven in the morning," Javi explained.

"Shit! We've got company," James shouted.

Alex heard that and flew out of the cabin to look at the radar. "What do you see, Captain?"

"Mr. C., there's a fast boat approaching from the southwest."

"Can you outrun it?" Alex asked, looking into the cabin with a concerned look.

"I'll see how much more I can get out of this baby. If we do, we may have to put in at the Keys for gas, 'cause I am not going to make it to Islamorada at this pace."

"How far out are we from Cuba?" I asked.

"We are well into international waters. If it's a Cuban gunboat, they have no business here," James replied.

"They'll do whatever they fucking want. Who is going to challenge them out here?" Javi said.

"The U.S. Navy would, Javier. Except they are not here," Alex replied.

"I don't know what kind of fucking engines they got but they are moving closer," Captain James retorted.

"We'll know if it's a gunboat when they take a shot at us."

"I gotta go east away from this asshole," Captain James said.

"Do what you need to do, Captain. Try and buy us a few more miles north.

I went downstairs to check on the ladies, particularly Jackie. She was looking a little better. They had placed some ice bags over her face, and the swelling had come down considerably. Plus, she had applied some makeup that Mel had given her and it made her feel much better. She inquired how things were going and I assured her and the others that everything would be fine. Just as I finished the sentence, a round hit in front of our boat missing our bow by maybe ten feet. From the sound, it could have been a 50-caliber. But who was counting? I ran out to the deck, only to see Big Bro a little frantic at the thought of getting shot at. "You OK, Bro?"

"Fuck, man, that was close," he replied.

Alex was back on the sat phone. Who the hell could he be talking to in the middle of this shit?

"Captain, do you see anything else on the radar?" asked Alex as he put the phone away.

"I do, Boss. I see another large vessel north and west of us," James replied.

"Great. Head for it now and fast!" Alex exclaimed.

"What do we have there, Boss?" I asked.

"It's good to have friends in high places, boys. That's the fucking U.S. Coast Guard to the rescue," he shouted as another round hit five feet off our starboard side.

"Hang on, boys," said James, as he blasted "Son of Sailor Man" by good old Jimmy over the twelve speakers he had on this tub... sorry... great fishing boat.

We were now closer to the Coast Guard vessel than we were to the Cuban gunboat. As we shortened the distance, a Coast Guard helicopter went right over our heads in the direction of the Cuban gunboat.

"Of course you would, asshole," said James, looking at

his radar.

"What's up?" I asked.

"One Cuban gunboat is returning home. That motherfucker got his finger up his ass and is hightailing it back to Cuba."

I was already opening the *cervesas* and passing them around. Plus, the special treat for the boys, Padrón Dámasos for Brother and me and the Family Reserves for Alex and La Puta.

Mel came out of the cabin, with a beer in one hand and motioning with the other for something.

"Where is my Padrón, *cabrón*?" she asked, looking at me and pretending to be upset.

"Yes!" Javi said. "I think a woman looks very sexy puffing on a cigar."

"I wonder why you think that, *Puta*," she replied, laughing and looking at Javi.

It was almost seven in the morning. The bright radiant sun was beginning to show its incredible yellow and orange rays, shooting out of the horizon with a light blue, whitewash backdrop of a sky. It was going to be a beautiful day in the Keys. We continued on toward the Coast Guard ship. As we went right by it, we waved and motioned our thanks to them. They in turn replied with a nice blast of their horn. It would be another hour to the tip of Key West where we would refuel and head back to the Bayside Marina at Worldwide Sportsman in Islamorada.

My plans had been to stay in Islamorada with Javi, Mel, and Jackie. Obviously, that had changed the moment we saw Jackie's condition. Alex confessed to me that if we all made it out in one piece from Cuba, he had planned to get married as soon as he could. He had wanted to do it at a Catholic church he knew in Marathon, but due to the unforeseen events he would wait for a better time.

So while we were happy to be back, we all suffered in our own way at the horrific torture endured by Jackie. The physical part would heal in time. We all knew that. But what about the mental suffering she undergone? We would have to wait and see. I had my hopes up since Mel had gone through similar treatment, and she was there to counsel Jackie. My Alpha team was damaged but not down and out. What we all needed now was sleep, rest, and relaxation. I was very proud of my big bro- at his professional behavior and demeanor under duress. Of course, I didn't think I noticed when he had to change his pants after the gunfire next to us. Or maybe, it was just saltwater that made them wet. Yeah, I'll go with that.

The sat phone rang and Alex picked it up. "Very well, Joey. We'll be putting in soon, and I'll call you back for more details. Keep digging, my boy. You're doing great."

"Now what?" I asked.

"Joey has been doing some digging into a case we are

working on. He was highly agitated by some information he uncovered," Alex replied. "Nothing I can do from here. I'll deal with it as soon as we get back to Islamorada."

CHAPTER THIRTY-THREE

New York City

Nikolas Akakios had satisfied his lust for Marta for the moment. After all these years of wanting her, Marta had allowed him back in her bed. It had been worth the wait. Thanks to his chemically enhanced libido, he had been able to perform quite admirably for the last two plus hours. Her lovemaking was an art, he thought. He would not be denied such a pleasure going forward.

Now he sat behind his desk in the den of his condominium. He could work from here as well as if he was back in his office. Within a few minutes, a conference call was about to start that could set up the future of the world order. Marta sat across from his desk on a leather sofa. She wore nothing but a see-through light baby blue silk robe. His secure phone rang. "Put it on speaker phone," she said.

"Gentlemen, I understand that everyone is on the call and that you are all on your secure phones," said a voice on the phone. "I'll dismiss with any pleasantries and get down to business. New York, can you bring us up to date?"

It was Akakios's turn to speak. "We are ready on our end. This morning we begin Phase One to be followed tomorrow morning, Eastern Standard Time, with Phase Two."

"Very well, New York. Is there anything that can

prevent or hamper your end of the operation?" the voice asked.

Akakios answered simply, "No."

"Phoenix, your turn," said the voice.

"All assets have been deployed and are in place. We are part of Phase Two for tomorrow morning," said another voice on the phone.

"Phoenix, you lost two assets in Brownsville, Texas. Any chance more will be lost?"

"Negative. We planned for that. We have eighteen available participants that are already in place."

"Shanghai, your report," said the voice.

It was General Dang's turn. "Our part of Phase One is ready to be executed today without any problems. Phase Two for tomorrow will also be executed without any delay."

"Beijing," said the voice.

"We are part of Phase Two and will begin our part through London selling the U.S. Treasury bonds in the open market as scheduled," said another voice.

"London?" asked the voice.

"We are ready to execute the sell orders as requested," said a voice in London.

"Japan, your turn."

"Our part is for tomorrow's Phase Two. We will call the Secretary of the Treasury as planned and begin demanding that they exchange hard assets for the U.S. government bonds."

Marta looked at Akakios with an inquisitive look. He motioned, rolling his right hand forward as if to say, "I'll explain later."

"Gentlemen, we are done here. All seems to be in order. We will not speak unless it is absolutely necessary until after the completion of both phases. Be well," said the voice as all the callers began hanging up their phones.

Akakios sat back in his chair and took a deep breath. The pill he had taken was still having some effects and he found himself with an erection as he looked at Marta's sensuous body across from him.

"Can you explain the part about hard assets?" she asked.

"I can do better than that. I can show you," he said as he took a position on the sofa facing up and softly pulled her face towards his hard asset.

"That's not what I meant," she said.

"But it is what I want," he retorted. He proceeded to pleasure himself with her magical mouth.

Moments later, she asked, "And how many pills did you take?"

Laughing, he replied, "Just the one."

"Next time, take a half," she said, somewhat seriously. "Now, tell me what Japan meant about exchanging hard assets for bonds."

"With the chaos we are about to unleash on the U.S. economy, the depression we are going to put her in, we want to add even more pressure. This crash is going to put a tremendous burden on the government. Creditors, such as China, Japan and others, are going to be fearful that the U.S. may not have the ability to pay back its debt. So slowly, one by one, our members in the cabal are going to be asking for collateral for the debt owed to them. Their fear will be that the full faith and credit of the U.S. Treasury is not enough to satisfy their debt. So, either pay me back now or secure this debt with hard assets, such as real estate, gold, etc."

"Ingenious. So China and Japan could end up owning the U.S."

"Not all of it. Naturally, there are a lot of assets in the hands of private ownership. I imagine those assets might go on a fire sale at some point. But yes, the U.S. is a very rich country in real estate. Think of the fields that they have neglected to explore and that are rich with oil, natural gas, and coal... all in the hands of countries starving for a source of energy, or better yet, all in the hands of our cabal. No other country in the world could rival our energy capabilities. Not Russia, not Saudi Arabia. No one."

"I know I've asked this before, but is your position secure in this cabal?'

"We all need each other. All for one, one for all.

Everyone is satisfied with how we have planned the distribution. Everyone has equal say in all decisions. I'm fine. We are fine. You know all this talk of grandiosity is making me hard again."

"Come here," she replied.

CHAPTER THIRTY-FOUR

Islamorada, Florida Keys

"Joey, we are back on land and everyone is safe," said Alex, as we all sat around, except for brother James, at a table at Zane Grey's bar on the second floor of Worldwide Sportsman Bayside Marina. "Tell me what you have found."

Joey went on explaining to Alex his findings about this character, Akakios or something.

We ordered another round of Bacardi mojitos and something to eat and brought out some new Padrons. We were just getting our land legs back. So many hours on a boat at the speeds we had been going had taken a toll on everyone. From my vantage point, I could see Big Bro below in his dock space, watering the boat down and being very animated with a few of his other captain friends. He was gesturing, as if to imitate a bird flying with one hand while still holding the hose with the other. He was going to be a happy camper from now on with that drone aboard.

A few minutes ago, I had reached Dan and Tom whom I had only left a day ago. Somehow it felt more like a month. They reported they had had no luck in securing any more of the men we had been looking for. The special task force was going to remain. However, their role, meaning Dan's and

Tom's, was being terminated. They were getting plane fare and a stipend to head home. Of course, I knew those muchachos were going to hang around Texas a little longer and find themselves a rodeo of some kind. Those SEALs work hard and play just as hard.

Alex completed his call and had a concerned look on his face. I handed him a cigar I had been saving for him. He took it, but I could see he was aloof, or perhaps he looked more pensive. "What's up, Boss?'

"I don't know what to make of it right now. We were investigating this company about possible insider trading and corporate espionage. Joey seems to think it is more than that," Alex replied.

"Joey is a bright kid, Boss. What's his thought?" I asked, looking around the table.

"He thinks the stock market trades, this hedge fund we are investigating, have taken a pattern of some kind, and he feels there is a lot more to it than just insider trading," he said, still with that pensive look on his face. "I can't figure it out."

"Who could you call? Know anyone at the SEC?"

"No, not at the SEC. I do know someone at the New York Stock Exchange," he replied.

"So, go for it," I said, as he looked up at me as if a light bulb had just gone off.

His cell phone rang and he got up and walked away to

answer the call. I looked around the table and noticed the mojitos were gone. Raising my hand, I said, “Nurse, we need more Bacardi mojitos, por favor.” It was breakfast time but who cared.

I was glad to see Jackie smiling and even enjoying her drink. She was slowly recovering, and hopefully none of what had happened to her would have a lasting effect. She worked for me and all, but I was beginning to be really concerned about her. Well, maybe concern was not the actual word. But, you know what? I was going with that for now.

Alex came back to the table, took his cigar, relit it, and after a long pull and exhale, he said, “That was my client Elo Teck. They have just been hacked and their top secret drone plans have been breached,” he said.

“Can they tell by whom? This guy, Akakios?” I asked.

“No, they think it is the Chinese government or some entity in China.”

“Really?” Julia said.

“They traced the hack back, or whatever you do, and found themselves going into a series of locations, some of which were in China.”

“That’s quite the coincidence of Akakios and now China going after the same company, Boss,” I said.

“What did you learn in tradecraft about coincidences, John?” Alex asked.

"No such thing."

"Exactly," he said.

"How about Joey? Can he help?" I asked.

"Already on it. I told Elo Teck to connect with Joey and give him access to what they did and what they found. Let him run with it and see what he can dig up. Meantime, I am calling my friend at the NYSE and see what he says."

I noticed a TV affixed to a wall, right by where we were sitting. I asked the waitress to turn it to a business channel. We all moved in a little closer as Alex moved away in order to make his call.

As the channel came on, there was a reporter with a microphone reporting from the floor of the NYSE. We turned the volume up to listen.

> *"... Repeating the top story for this morning. With minutes before the bell rings here for opening of trading, the NYSE has cancelled the trading of three stocks that seemed to have been the target of a cyber attack this morning and/or last night: Elo Teck, SunMarc Bank, and Super Stores. Trading on these stocks and/or their derivatives has been suspended until further notice. A full investigation is under way by ––"*

Alex came back and started telling us what his friend at the

NYSE told him, which was the same we had heard on the TV. This was bigger than just an insider-trading incident.

"What the news media is not reporting yet," Alex said, "is that the New York Stock Exchange has found a series of trades, in what is called the futures market, that are very suspicious. Large orders going in through dark pools to sell, then canceled before they are executed."

"Boss, you are talking Chinese to us, pardon the pun," I replied, as Julia smiled.

"Dark pools are set up to add liquidity to large selling volume of individual stocks; however, the problem is that the seller or buyer is not identified," Julia explained. "If word gets out about the intended buy or sell, then it can exacerbate the activity on the stock and its derivatives."

"I think I need another mojito. I don't want to make light of this, but both of you guys are talking above my pay grade," I said.

"Understood, John. The bottom line is that someone, perhaps more than one entity, is manipulating the markets. Obviously, the hacking of these three publicly traded companies was intended to drive the price down and at the same time breach secure information these companies have about their business and customers."

"OK. I am starting to follow. So, when trading in these stocks resumes, it is very likely the price will drop due to the news about them. How does that help an investor?" I asked.

"You can make money on a stock trade by selling 'short.' In other words, you can sell a stock before you buy it, hoping the price goes down. Then, when you feel the drop is sufficient, you buy the stock at a lower price. Basically, you bought low and sold high. Just in reverse order," Julia explained.

"Well, I guess we all have our areas of expertise and mine is not the same as yours. But I get the drift." I think I understood, but after being up over twenty-four hours without sleep, I was a bit punchy. Our adrenaline rush had lasted quite a long time after the operation in Cuba. Now, between the Bacardi and cigars, I was coming down from it at last and really needed some sleep.

"There is a full investigation starting on all these dark pool trades by the NYSE, and they have called in the FBI," said Alex. "Interestingly enough, Joey had traced some of these trades to the hedge fund owned and managed by Akakios."

"Did you report that to your friend at NYSE?" Julia asked.

"Not in so many words. After all, what Joey was doing is not necessarily sanctioned or legal. I just said we had been poking around and suggested they look into our friend," Alex replied.

"So now what, Boss?" I asked.

"I need to get back to Chicago with Julia. Jackie needs

to get medical attention back home. You, Javi, and Mel can hang out if you like. I can call for you if I need you," the boss replied.

"I would like to go back with you guys and stay with Jackie," Mel said as Jackie smiled at her.

"Perfect. I'll take the SUV back to Homestead Air Force Base and arrange for a ride back as I drive. John, you and Javi secure our equipment here. Rent a car, and I'll arrange for your flight back when you are ready. Does that work for you guys?" Alex asked.

"We are good, Boss. I am sure Javi and I will find something to do. Perhaps we can actually go fishing with Big Bro. If there is anything we can do about this new development, please give us a call."

"I will, John. Please thank Captain James for his participation. I will make sure he is compensated properly," Alex said looking down to the dock area where James was.

"I think he's ahead of you on that."

"What do you mean?"

"Nothing really. I don't think he is looking for monetary payment of any kind. He was happy to help and be part of the team."

Alex smiled. "I hope he doesn't get too big an advantage on the other fishing captains."

"Right," I said, returning the smile back at Alex.

Javi and I helped Alex, Julia, and Jackie get ready to

leave. My mind was strictly set on sleeping for the next twenty-four hours. I am sure Big Bro could find a place for Javi and me me to crash.

CHAPTER THIRTY- FIVE

Chicago, Illinois

Alex, Julia, Jackie, and Mel had flown out of Homestead Air Force Base in a private plane provided by Elo Teck, Alex's client. They were under contract to the DOD so getting clearance to leave from the base had not been an issue. Upon arrival in Chicago, Jackie had been admitted into Northwestern Medical Center for observation, a full checkup, and any procedures required. Mel accompanied her and made arrangements to stay in the private hospital room for as long as Jackie would be there.

Alex and Julia had a quiet and restful night. Their conversation had avoided any replay of the events that occurred in Cuba. Andy Anderson, Julia's partner, had visited them briefly at their home.

On schedule, Alex arrived at his office at six in the morning. Joy, his assistant, was there to greet him with a huge hug. She had coffee ready and had opened the curtains in the office so that Alex could enjoy the sunrise over Lake Michigan, as he did every day from his beautiful vantage point.

"Is Joey here yet?" Alex asked.

"He is in his office and will be here in five minutes. I told him to give you a chance to acclimate yourself first,"

Joy replied. "Mr. C., we've all prayed for you and Julia and the others to return safely. We are happy you are all back in one piece."

"Thank you, Joy. We appreciate that. I just hope Jackie can recover both physically and mentally. The rest of us will be fine," Alex said as Joey walked into the office. "Kid, what you got for me?"

Joey flashed those bright white teeth of his in the biggest smile possible, as he walked over and hugged Alex, holding on for a couple of seconds. "Mr. C., happy to see you."

"Happy to be seen. Let's get down to business."

Joey began, "I spoke to Elo Teck's top IT guy yesterday after our conversation. I was able to identify some of the IP addresses used in the hacking. All very elaborate. However, they left themselves open in one occurrence, and unquestionably China is the place of origination of the hacks."

"Do you think that the other two companies, SunMarc Bank and Super Stores, are targets of the same hacking group?"

"If I was a betting man, and I am not, I would say, yes. Too much coincidence here."

"When you say China, can you tell if it's a Chinese group or the Chinese government?"

"No, I cannot. I did trace it to Shanghai, though."

"Well, it makes no difference at this point. There is an orchestrated effort to breach these companies' databases and at the same time benefit from their price drop in the stock market."

"I was told yesterday that they were able to get Elo Teck's plan for the DOD's drone project. That is scary that a foreign group or government got access to our government's secret defense projects."

"It is. But Elo Teck built in a series of faults in their plans just in case something like this happened. So what they stole are plans that will not result in the actual final product. If they build it as per the plans they got it will never fly."

"That's a smart move."

"Yeah, well, they still have a lot of information they should not have."

Alex was racking his brain trying to figure out the objective here. Something was not sitting well, and he was having an uneasy feeling about the whole thing. He called Special Agent in Charge Casselback and inquired about their efforts to apprehend the remaining eighteen men that had eluded them from Mexico to Texas. After Alex brought him up to date on his adventures in Cuba without details, Casselback had no good news for him. The FBI special task force was still deployed on the Texas border. Casselback explained that the potential attack on a shopping mall had led to nothing. They had no other leads and the men in custody had not provided any worthwhile intelligence.

"I was not aware that there was the threat of an attack on a mall," said Alex.

"Your John Powers uncovered that when he questioned one of the men we apprehended," Casselback replied.

"Right. We never spoke about what he was doing with you. We were kind of busy with our problems."

"Understood. So, yes, there was a plan to attack a mall. We don't know when or where. We do, however, think that the other potential terrorists do not have malls as their targets. I think they divested their targets just in case we caught some of them."

"Got it. I will call you back if I think of anything. Please call me the moment you have any other leads. It is very important. And, thank you."

"Alex, thank you. I will call and I am delighted to hear everyone made it out of Cuba."

Alex sat back, trying to put the pieces together. He was not sure if there were any pieces to put together. Joey walked back in with a large whiteboard on wheels.

"What are you doing?"

"Boss, I like to use a whiteboard like this to think out loud. It's similar to what the police or detectives use on those TV shows to pin pictures or write stuff about the case. You sit there and start thinking out loud. I'll start building a puzzle here, and maybe we can put this thing together."

So they began writing things on this whiteboard, similar to throwing garbage on a wall and seeing what sticks.

Joy walked into the office and went straight to Alex's large TV above a credenza behind his desk.

"What's going on?" Alex asked.

"Watch," Joy replied, as Joey took a seat in front of Alex's desk.

There was a scene of chaos in front of some office buildings that were not readily identifiable. Police crime scene tape surrounded a large area, and smoke was visible from inside the buildings.

"We have had reports of additional explosions in various parts of the country. What you are seeing is the Chicago Mercantile Exchange where multiple explosions have occurred in the last few minutes. As of now, we do not have any information on who or how many may be hurt. We will remain here and update these events. In the meantime let's join my colleague, Ashley, reporting from New York City at the New York Stock Exchange."

"Thank you, Mark. We are standing at the corner of Broad and Wall Street, just a few hundred feet from

where explosions rocked the city this morning as hundreds of employees who work on the exchange were making their way in. At least three explosives went off on the street. Many have been injured, and some are feared dead in this horrific and what seems to be coordinated attack on our nation's financial systems. We have been unable to get official word from anyone in authority at this point, as everything seems to be happening at a maddening pace. Let's break away to Minneapolis, Minnesota, where my colleague, Peter, is standing by in yet another attack."

"Thank you, Ashley. Behind me is the Mall of the Americas, considered by many as the largest mall in the United States. This mall accommodates more than five hundred stores in over three million square feet of space. Within minutes of the attack on the Mercantile and New York exchanges, a series of explosions were set off in this mall at various locations. They were choreographed in such a way that shoppers were made to run from one direction into another, as the explosions followed them, seemingly to maximize casualties or injuries. Many are saying the attacks here are because of the symbolic name of the mall, Mall of the Americas. This is --"

Alex lowered the volume. He couldn't take any more.

Joy and Joey sat there, stunned at what they were witnessing.

"Joy, please get Tom Ridge on the phone. It's going to be hard to get him. Make sure you tell them who is calling and that I have information about what is going on," Alex instructed. "Also, get me Mr. Allan Reese, assistant to the Chairman of the New York exchange."

"Joey, your whiteboard is spectacular. Let's write a few more things as I see them." Alex kept throwing things out for Joey to write. Soon a picture was developing as the board filled up with events that had occurred and were occurring as they wrote them. Alex said, "This country is still mourning the loss of over three thousand souls from the attacks of 9/11. Why is this happening?" It was a rhetorical question. Joey, the only person with him, had no answers. Neither did Alex.

Joy walked into his office. "Mr. C., I have Mr. Ridge on line one and Mr. Reese on line two."

"Thank you, Joy. I am going to pick up Ridge first, and then I want to conference in Reese."

"Very well, let me know when."

Alex winked back at Joy and motioned to her with his right hand that he needed some water as he picked up the phone with his left. He then motioned to Joey to sit down, pointing to the couch in front of his desk.

"Tom, thank you for picking up. I know how busy you

are. I have Allan Reese from the New York exchange on the other line. I want your permission to put him on with us."

"Go right ahead, Alex," replied Ridge.

"Allan, thank you for taking my call. I have the Assistant to the President for Homeland Security, Mr. Tom Ridge on the line with us."

No one exchanged pleasantries. It was all business.

"Gentlemen, let me get to the point. Due to various operations and/or cases we have been working, my team and I have put together a possible scenario for today's events," Alex said, as Joey perked up when he heard "my team and I." "In any case, I have reason to believe that a coordinated cyber attack on our financial markets and a terrorist attack on our nation are being orchestrated by individuals in our country in conjunction with Chinese interests. While I have no solid proof, we do have circumstantial evidence that ties all this together."

"What are you recommending, Alex?" asked Ridge.

"My first suggestion is that we close all financial markets from trading. All of them. Secure the physical plant immediately, as they may be targets of more attacks. Secondly, Tom, I think your department or the FBI needs to pay an immediate visit to Nikolas Akakios in New York City and let him know that we know. Furthermore, he needs to make sure that all attacks, cyber and physical, cease immediately or his next stop will be one of our extradition partner countries for added serious questioning."

"Do you have any proof about Akakios?" asked Ridge.

"Before we get into that—this is Allan Reese by the way—I am going to go with Alex's suggestion on my end and alert all the exchanges to close immediately. Mr. Ridge, it would help if I can say that you strongly advise we do that, sir."

"Done, Allan," Ridge replied.

"Very well. Thank you both. If you don't mind, I am going to get off the phone and take care of business. Hopefully, we'll meet under better circumstances next time," Reese said.

"So, Tom, what do you think?"

"I would like to have solid proof if—"

Alex interrupted. "Sir, I am not asking for you to arrest Akakios. If he is not guilty, then nothing will change today, and whatever plans they have will continue to occur during the day. However, if he is a little bit involved, I think you can put the fear of God in him and tell him, while we have no proof, we are building a case and all attacks must stop immediately."

"He could call our bluff and do nothing," Ridge said.

"Agreed. However, I think there are other major parties in this endeavor that he is going to have to call, and who would rather lose a battle and be left alive to fight another day. Akakios could be a casualty of this battle, much like the two guys we apprehended under the tunnel. Tom, I think this war is bigger than we think."

"Very well, Alex. I can't disagree with the strategy. Akakios will be visited within the next fifteen minutes in New York. Let's hope you are right and he can somehow stop these shocking attacks on our homeland. Thank you."

"Thank you, Tom."

Alex looked at Joey who had been sitting there listening to this whole thing. He could not help to recognize that Joey was totally flabbergasted by the discussion. Alex smiled and felt somewhat relieved that perhaps other attacks would cease. The whiteboard had worked, but only because they had accidentally been involved in various parts of the puzzle and they were able to put it together.

CHAPTER THIRTY-SIX
Chicago, Illinois

I returned from Islamorada last night. The events that had taken place while I was sleeping in the Keys were atrocious. By the grace of God, the casualty count had been minimal. Only three people had died from the three attacks combined: one at the Chicago Mercantile Exchange, two in the Mall of the Americas in Minneapolis, and none at the New York Stock Exchange. Many injuries, but none serious, had been reported. Two terrorists were apprehended in Minneapolis. Unfortunately, just like the two in Mexico, very little information was retrieved from either of them.

Alex gave us a briefing this morning and brought us all up to date. It turned out that agents of both the FBI and Homeland Security visited Nikolas Akakios. I didn't ask if they were special agents. Under the circumstances, I didn't think being a smart-ass was appropriate at the moment. Akakios, Alex had been told, was quiet and serene without taking the accusations personally. He knew they had no proof; otherwise he would have been arrested and charged. So, he played it very cool and just listened to the assumptions they were making. The fact was both the cyber attacks and the terrorist attacks stopped that same day. Akakios was told not to leave the country, and I was sure the courts approved all types of wiretaps and whatever other forms of surveillance were available to place on this person. They should order a colonoscopy and place a bug up his ass, if you asked me. But, they were not asking, so let me go on.

The State Department contacted their counterpart in China. Using the same argument they used on Akakios, they were told by Chinese officials that a rogue team of cyber security personnel, under the direction of Director Wáng, was found to have breached the U.S. companies' databases. They apologized and agreed to destroy any and all material uncovered in their investigation. Furthermore, the individual in charge of this team was found guilty of insurrection and threatening the security of the country and was executed in front of a firing squad. I said, yeah, right.

Jackie was much better, both physically and mentally. Mel's assistance and constant companionship had made a big difference. We all felt that she would recover fully and be her fiery self again soon.

Big Brother Captain James found that he had no clue as to how to fly the drone, and none of us had stayed around long enough to teach him. Not that Javi or I could for that matter. So he was offering free fishing charters and all the beer they could drink to Mel and Jackie if they would return and show him how to fly the little bird. His secret advantage for catching dolphins and tunas was not deployed as of yet.

Yours truly was enjoying the weather in Chicago before things got really cold. I was planning a trip to visit my godson, Ian, and his mother, Ellen, in Boulder, Colorado, but I had no intention of going in the winter months. As a matter of fact, my plan was to go back to sunny Florida and Islamorada again. Something our waitress said privately to me as we left Zane Grey's bar that day we were all together, stayed with me. "I love catching big ones," she said. The lady might be quite the fishing expert, but we would see.

As they say in the news business, stay tuned for more.

THE END

About Owen Parr

Thank you for reading Operation Black Swan.

I was born in Havana, Cuba, a few years before my country of birth, which by the way, was known as "The Pearl of the Caribbean" prior to the sorrow and suffering that set in, became a communist-dictatorship under the Castro brothers. That era is known as Cuba BC, "Before Castro."

In 1959 my father and mother left everything behind and we moved to the United States. It is interesting to note, before you say, "Owen Parr" a Cuban?" That, my dad, Owen Parr, was born in New York and his dad moved to Havana when my dad was eight years old.

Moving on, I grew up in Miami Beach, finished my elementary education at St. Joseph's and attended high school at St. Patrick's, both in Miami Beach and obviously Catholic schools. After high school, I began college seeking a career in Electrical Engineering. Mr. Parr, my dad, was a Civil engineer and had wanted me to study engineering. My two older brothers had declined that invitation, so I felt duty bound to comply with his wishes.

For six years I worked in the engineering department of our local utility, Florida Power and Light. Bored to death, I opened a side business during the construction boom in South Florida, circa 1970's and sold floor coverings and appliances to builders for their newly constructed homes and condominiums. This was the time in Miami when the so-called "drug-wars" began, lasting through the 1980's.

I consolidated my efforts by selling my part-time business to my partner and left FP&L to get into real estate sales full-time. Four years later, I opened my own real estate company and grew it to five offices with over one hundred associates and a real estate school. In my thirties and in the middle of a personal boom, interest rates for mortgages climbed to 19%, with the Prime Rate at 21%, as Jimmy Carter left and Ronald Reagan became president. No one, I mean, no one bought homes at that point. So, I sold my real estate company for a minuscule fraction of what it had been worth and moved on.

In 1986, just prior to the stock market crash of 1987, I became a financial advisor with a major Wall Street firm. Proud to say, I swam up-stream and almost thirty years later I am still at it and enjoying it tremendously. Taking care of my clients is paramount. Today, I enjoy a partnership in my business with an associate that will cater to my client's sons and daughters. You're asking, when did you start writing? That's what we want to know. Right?

All through my career I wrote. Newsletters at the jobs, advertising campaigns, and articles for trade magazines and so on. In the 1990's I developed an itch to write screenplays. When to school and took a few courses and yes, I wrote two screenplays and outlined three others. Actually pitched "Due Diligence" the screenplay, personally to Oliver Stone. He loved the name, but did not care for the screenplay or the politics within it. I enjoyed the learning experience.

Last year I took courses on writing fiction and began converting my screenplays into action, suspense, and fictional novels. Due Diligence being the first. "Operation Black Swan," release date November 2015, "The Dead Have Secrets" and "States United," to follow.

If you see me out and about, you'll see me asking for a table for ten, to accommodate my lovely wife of 48, whom I married 48 years ago. My lovely daughters; Ingrid and Astrid, with my beautiful grandchildren; Robbie, Logan, Dylan and Cameron. Did I say 'ten'? I did, need room for my two buddies and best friends, Jose and Todd, the son in laws.

They always say, "Write what you know." My multiple plotted international political suspense thrillers with global backgrounds come from what I know. I love writing them; I trust you'll love reading them. When I read fiction, I want the author through his plot and characters, to make me part of the story. My goal in writing is to entertain the reader, to sweep you away to the locations I write about and put you in the story, together with my characters. Enough of this. Go read one of my books! Oh, and thank you.

Acknowledgements

First and foremost I want to recognize and thank my wife Ingrid. This year we celebrated our 48th wedding anniversary. Her patience and understanding knows no bounds. When I am involved with a new manuscript I tend to get a little absent-minded and the "honey-do" list gets left behind. She is my secret weapon.

All my friends and yes fans, for supporting me and putting up with my constant barrages of promotion via e-mails, Facebook, twitter and all the other social media I employ to get the word out.

My friend, Tom Spencer, Esquire. He is my consigliore, confidant and source for many of my tradecraft ideas. He is always willing to listen and offer constructive critique.

Captain James Chappell, owner and operator of "catchollatofish" Fishing Charters, out of Bayside Marina in Islamorada, Florida. For allowing me to use his real name and assisting with various nautical facts. I heard he might buy a drone.

Mrs. Phyllis Cox, with Writers Digest University and Mrs. Roxanna Adams, of Five Star Editing. These ladies have been invaluable in converting my Spanglish into something you all can read.

My partner, at my day job, Frank Murillo. And assistants: Tatianna Martinez and Alberto Bravo, for picking up the slack. (Don’t tell our boss).

Finally, fellow best selling independent authors for their mentorship, friendship and constant inspiration, namely: Mike Pettit and Joe Broadmeadow.

Preview

The Dead Have Secrets
A John Powers Novel

By
Owen Parr

Chapter One

The winds were howling and pounding the front side of the small but quaint A-framed home. The snow piled up two feet high as the snowstorm that moved in the evening was relentlessly causing havoc in the town of Boulder, Colorado. The temperature was below freezing and the only visible things surrounding the home were the Aspen trees that had endured many snowstorms before and yet stood erect defying the wind and the snow. The snow-covered ground was a mixture of dirty white snow, littered with broken down brown branches, some leaves that had survived the fall season and whatever rubbish had been around. The homes were sparsely located in this area just west of the "Chautauqua State Park" on a road headed west to a town called Netherlands. On a clear day the view from the second story's mater bedroom of the home was magnificent. The east side of the Green Mountains is called the Flatirons due to its unique rock formation. At just over eight thousand feet in elevation, the Flatirons formed a sharp and distinct contrast to the city of Boulder just below and to the east.

Three men, wearing snow masks, slowly climbed the steep embankment from the road leading to the home. Their hunter-like camouflaged attires blended well with the elements. Hardly visible, were their sawed-off shotguns. On a normal night, they would have looked out of place. But this evening, no one was around to see them. Visibility was near zero as the snowstorm and wind created a grey haze that obscured the scenery. They continued their slow and deliberate climb with an aspect of professionals, not amateur hunters.

Casey McBride read in bed. Occasionally she would look to her left and see her son, Ian, sleeping like an angel. His bright big green eyes were resting now. She caressed his red hair with her left hand and followed it with a sigh and some tears. Ian had worshipped his father, Braden, and Casey had not been able to sense fully explain to Ian, why his dad had perished in Afghanistan. Eight-year-old children had no understanding of war or human conflicts of this nature. Why should they? She thought.

Captain Braden McBride had been a hero. His service to his country had been a duty and a dream he had successfully achieved. His death, however, had been untimely, as is every death in war. His bravery and dedication to duty was something Casey hoped Ian would inherit from his dad. There would be a time for Ian to understand not only death, but also his own father's.

Amidst the constant sound of the howling wind and the snow battering the roof and ceiling to floor windows, Casey heard a creaking sound she knew too well. The wooden stairs leading from the living room to the bedrooms upstairs had a definite sound to them as you reached the landing, midway up.

Turning off the light on night table she moved swiftly, locked her bedroom door and bundled up Ian in a blanket and carried him into the bathroom. She laid Ian, still asleep, in the bathtub resting his head in a pillow. Following her instincts after closing the bathroom door, she quickly went into her walk-in closet and reached for Braden's gun case that was stored high in a shelve above her hanging clothes. She knew how to use the weapons, but her heart was beating so loudly, all she could think of was calming down enough, so she could effectively protect he son and herself from what she perceived as an imminent danger. To her, it seemed she was taking forever to open the gun case. Seconds seemed like minutes, her hands trembled as she finally opened the case.

Someone was trying to open the door to her bedroom. She tried warning the intruder by calling out, but no sound came out as she screamed the warning. She heard a second sound from downstairs as if someone had knocked down a table. She now knew that there was more than one person in her house. With her back to the wall, she slid down to the floor and sat holding a Beretta A400 Xtreme Unico Semi-Auto Shotgun that had been Braden's favorite for duck hunting. It was loaded with three and a half inch shells and it could fire four rounds in less than one minute.

She heard someone's voice. She was momentarily confused. Where the intruders someone she knew? But, why come unannounced? She heard the voice again. It was Ian calling for her from the bathroom. She could not wait to allow the intruders to walk in her bedroom. Ian began walking out of the bathroom into a dark room. What is going on? She asked herself.

The moment she asked herself that question, it all became clear. As if someone had said, sit back and let me explain.

She had little time to think; the door to her room was being forcefully opened...

To contact author, write him at:

owen@owenparr.com

Made in the USA
Middletown, DE
08 June 2016